THE COVEN'S CURSE

THE COVEN'S CURSE

JAMIE LEE FRY

BIGMOUNTAIN PUBLISHING

BOOK THREE OF
THE DARK MAGIC SERIES:
THE COVEN'S CURSE
JAMIE LEE FRY

Print edition ISBN: 9798988215639
E-book edition ISBN: 9798988215622
Barnes & Noble Edition ISBN: 9798988215646

First edition: April 2024
10 9 8 7 6 5 4 3 2 1

WWW.AUTHORJAMIELEEFRY.COM

This is a work of fiction. Names, characters, places, and incidents either are the product of the author's imagination or are used fictitiously, and any resemblance to actual persons, living or dead, business establishments, events or locales is entirely coincidental.

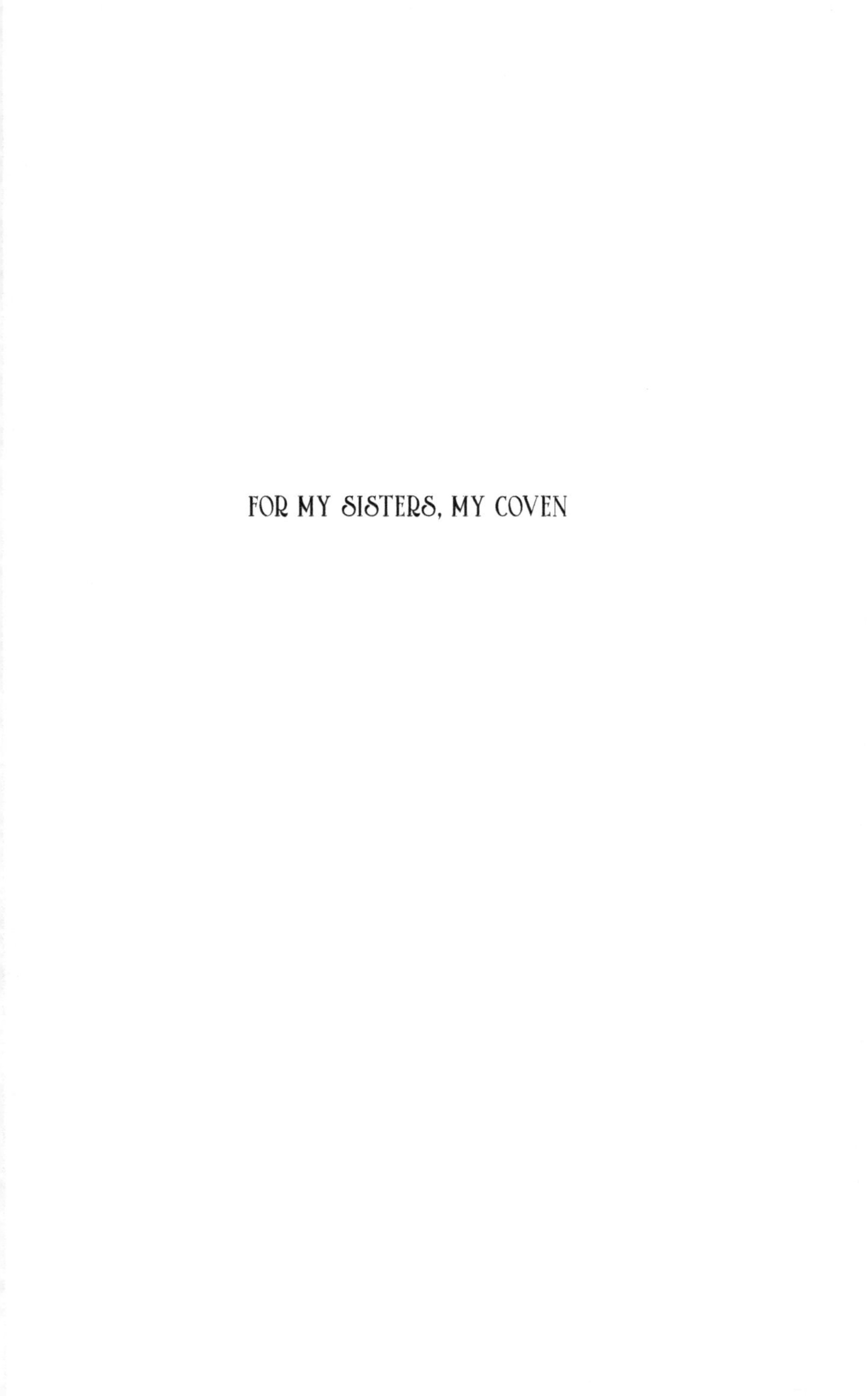

FOR MY SISTERS, MY COVEN

PROLOGUE
AFTER THE FOREST

Everything hurts.

My heart.

My soul.

My hand.

I grit my teeth and focus on the sound of my breathing to distract myself from the intense pain. I wince as crimson flows down my palm. The metallic scent of blood stings my nostrils.

Desperate times.

Using all my strength, I squeeze out every last drop, filling the shallow black bowl below me. My eyes stay fixed as the drops fall one by one, each creating a ripple in the red mixture. It's almost hypnotic.

Callen would kill me if he saw me using a kitchen knife again. But Callen's not here.

The floorboards let out a loud groan as I stretch to reach the first aid kit outside of my circle. I came prepared. I knew my offering would have to be significant. With precision, I wrap my hand in white gauze, while memorizing the spell I crafted.

This has to work.

I don't know what else to do.

I take my time lighting my new black candles, the ones I purchased today from the shop in town on my way home from school. With each one, I make a small plea to the universe. The flames dance in the stillness of the attic as if obeying my request. Shadows flicker along the walls as I move about, ready to take my place—alone.

Here goes nothing.

With a mindful breath, I attempt to let go of the words that haunt me—those awful words that stripped away my magic, the very ones that are embedded in my brain and on rampant repeat. When the rival coven was chanting their incantation, I couldn't make out what they were saying, but now the chant is clear as day as if intentional—a residual effect of their spell— *Tenebras invocamus. Expellant magicae ad infernos.*

They not only rid us of our magic, but also left their mark by slowly driving me insane. *Tenebras invocamus. Expellant magicae ad infernos.*

Ugh! Get out of my head.

I can't have their words messing with my plan. I must calm my mind and get a clear image—it's the only way.

Dropping to the middle of my circle, I cross my legs, feeling the roughness of the floor against my skin. I take a deep breath and prepare myself for what's to come, hoping my plea will be heard, for this is my last chance to save Riley. Tomorrow, he turns eighteen, and the transformation will be complete. I may be a fool for trying, but it's all I've got. We've already lost so much. I can't let the curses win.

All right, Izzy. Be strong. You got this.

As I focus on each element, my body trembles with the power of my imagination—not my magic. I visualize my coven, united and healthy, with the hum of powerful forces emanating from us. I picture Tahlia with tears of joy, knowing she escaped her possible fate. I can almost feel Riley's loving embrace as he scoops me into his arms, thanking me for saving him from his wretched curse. The sense of satisfaction is almost too real. My cheeks involuntarily lift as a smile tugs at each corner of my lips.

After letting the visions resonate for a few minutes, I'm ready to recite my spell.

Here goes nothing.

"Hail to the guardians of mother earth, air, fire, and water.

Hear my plea.

I ask for your help to invoke thee,

For my magic is gone.

Bring it back to where it belongs.

I ask of my guardian to bring me my fire.

Restore it from the liar.

Help your sister witch.

Bring my coven back to full rich.

My final plea, and please let it be.

Break my love from his anomaly.

I lay it all out there for thee.

Please share and give love for all eternity."

I repeat the chant three times, my voice rising and falling in perfect rhythm with the beat of my heart. I take a deep breath, savoring the feeling of hope that still lingers in the air before closing out the spell.

"So shall it be."

I close my eyes and let my senses take over, feeling the hot air lick my skin, listening for a voice to guide me, waiting for my fire to rage once again.

Nothing.

Fat tears swallow my eyes before cascading down my cheeks.

"No, this can't be it. Please. I beg you to help me. Anyone who's listening. Please. I'm trying. I need my coven to be whole again. I want my magic. I want Riley."

I wait hollowly, feeling the emptiness growing inside of me. The rustling of the trees against the house creates a sense of unease as the sky outside grows darker with each passing second, ready to swallow me whole.

Silence. Stillness. Darkness.

I feel nothing.

Emotional pain carves its way through my body in jagged patterns, ripping me to shreds from the inside out.

Defeated, I blow out the candles, my breath catching in my throat with each one. I scoop up the spellbook and Isobel's diary, leaving everything else as is.

A sense of finality washes over me as I lock the door and slip the key into its place. The tiny wooden steps creak under my weight as I slug down them in total darkness, wondering if I will ever need that room again.

I carefully set my items down into the hide-a-hole and replace the floorboards.

Nearing the doorway, exiting the third floor, I catch a glimpse over my right shoulder—something moved.

Hope.

I spin around, facing the shadowy room. My fingers walk across the wall, searching for the light switch.

"Hello?"

All I can hear is the steady beat of my heart, pumping loudly in my ears, drowning everything else out.

"Anna? Isobel?"

I find the light and flick it upward. My eyes take a moment to focus.

There's nothing there.

For a moment, I wonder if I wishfully imagined the movement, hoping for my fallen family to guide me once again.

I miss them.

Making my way toward the doorway, I glance once more over my shoulder. Saddened, I reach out and click the light switch off. The room slowly tunnels into darkness again. As the door latches behind me, I twist around, letting my gaze fall on the unique flaws and imperfections in the old wood, hoping if I linger a moment longer, something will happen. But nothing happens.

Just my imagination—right?

CHAPTER 01
OCTOBER

I'm drenched in sweat, my pajamas clinging to me like a second layer of skin. Every night when I close my eyes, the same nightmare awaits me. I'm transported back to that day in the forest. The haunting images are etched deeply into my brain, refusing to be forgotten.

We failed.

Five people died that day.

That's not something you can come back from.

Death never gets easier. The pain is a constant companion that weighs me down like an unwanted suit of armor.

How have I endured so much loss? The question nearly paralyzes me, making me a prisoner in my bed.

Perhaps Mrs. Jamison was right about me. I'm cursed, not only as a witch, but in my life in general. Bad luck always finds me, no matter where I go. There is no such thing as a fresh start. I was foolish to believe that things would be better in East Gate. It's painful to think about all the death that's consumed me in such a short amount of time.

Eight people—eight murders—*eight*. That's only since

May. First, I watched my frenemy, Sondra, fall—well, she was pushed to her death. Then, we hit Megan with Jessa's Jeep and left her to die on the cold, dark pavement like some kind of roadkill. I'm now left to deal with the consequences of our actions. Officer Tim, who was my friend, then sudden enemy, stabbed my Grandma Anna in the heart. Mia, Margo's mom, was murdered by the rival coven. Bree, Tim, and Sid took care of the rivals by murdering Mrs. Jamison and her three cohorts, whose names I found out later were Robin, Dale, and Darla.

Dale and Darla were brother and sister—go figure. Their creepy, murdering, witchy ways ran in the family. The siblings owned Invoke Awakenings together, and so far, no one has questioned their absence as far as I know. The only people who would miss them are dead. But that's all the information I've been given on the robed rivals, and I have so many questions.

Bree, Barrett, Tim, and Sid are working on things, but they don't give us much information. I hate being kept in the dark. I know they're trying to protect us, but I don't need protection.

I need answers.

It's hard to believe how much our world has changed in such a short time, including Tim's behavior. He went from being my friend to an enemy and back to being an ally within a matter of a week. The continuous back and forth has left me disoriented. It's hard to keep track of which version of Tim I'll face each day. Fortunately, I don't have to interact with him much as the adults supposedly have things 'under control.' But I'm not one to sit back and entrust my fate to someone else—especially if half of them are the very thing I'm trying to destroy.

But the rival coven—they ruined everything.

Everything!

Because of them, we have no chance left in hell of breaking the hunter's curse. We have no magic left in us. How can you break a magical curse without magic?

You can't.

I've tried.

They stripped our bloodline birthright away before we even knew what was coming—their stupid chant—*Tenebras invocamus. Expellant magicae ad infernos.* I still can't get it out of my head.

What made them more powerful than us?

Was it the dark magic?

Was it them channeling their dark mother, Elizabeth Crowley?

I don't know if I'll ever get the answers I seek.

What I do know is that I hate them.

Because of them, my nightmares always end the same. Riley's cold blue eyes tearing through my soul, leaving me raw, broken, and alone. They're the reason I have hate in my heart. Because of them, we're still fair game, and it's always hunting season. We have no way of defending ourselves. The rival coven robbed us of our arsenal—our magic. Witch-on-witch crime should be a sin. But I guess it's all covens for themselves, which is a terrifying thought.

We have no idea how many hunters or opposing covens are lurking in the darkness, ready to eliminate us. Hunters want to kill us because it's their duty—their curse. Other covens presumably want us dead, so they will be liberated from the hunters that our bloodline burdened them with. I can't help but imagine that if all witches near and far pooled our powers, we could do the unthinkable and break the curse once and for all, but people don't just wear a badge that says, *hi, I'm a witch; want to play magic?*

Life is never that easy, is it?

If it were, I wouldn't have been caught off guard by Mrs. Jamison.

Plus, it's not like the hunters would give up their birthright without a fight. Tim made sure we understood that when he came to our rescue. It was more for his self-preservation than for our safety. Upon the death of the final bloodline witch, their legacy will cease to exist. It's a double-edged sword— one more of Elizabeth Crowley's devious deceptions.

And the icing on the big, fat, rival coven cake—my sweet friend Margo would have remained ignorant of the truth surrounding her girlfriend's death if it weren't for them. Our friendship's survival and our coven's survival, for that matter, depended on that secret staying locked up tight.

They ruined us.

Tahlia and Margo still have each other, though. The Latham-Harts took Margo in for the time being. Since we couldn't glamour Mia's wounds, we made it look like she skipped town, leaving her daughter behind. Margo is always on the losing end of things. I wish there were a way to make things better, but you can't bring people back from the dead without consequences. We know this firsthand.

As for Jessa and me, we've been shunned. Jessa remains in denial that she had anything to do with Megan's death. She claims the rival coven didn't know what they were talking about, but Callen and I know the truth, so she keeps her distance from us.

Our group is broken, and so is my heart.

I miss my friends.

I miss the way things used to be.

After that day in the forest, I should have known we could never go back to how things were. I lied to Margo to protect her—to protect my coven—to protect Jessa.

Did I make a mistake?

Maybe.

Lying in bed rehashing things won't get me anywhere, but this morning is no different from the last thirty-seven days.

Not that I'm counting or anything.

I stretch my arms and legs, shedding the weight of my problems that keep me pinned to my bed. With a heavy sigh, I turn over and grab my phone, knowing the only notification waiting for me is from Callen. He's the only one who texts me these days. Nevertheless, I can't help but feel a twinge of excitement when I see the little notification bubble, hoping today might be different. However, my excitement quickly fades away when I realize it's just another message from Callen, my only friend.

Callen: Good morning, sunshine! I'd bet my life savings that you're still in bed. GET UP!

I slowly shift my gaze to my toes, which have barely made their way out from under the blankets—the closest I've come to getting out of bed.

Dang it. He knows me too well.

Izzy: I think someone's had a little too much espresso this morning. How many times do I need to tell you? Only one shot before 9 a.m. And you're wrong. I've been up for hours.

Callen: Liar! :)

Izzy: Not going to respond to that. Anyway, what's up?

While I await Callen's response, I pull my covers over my head and my mind drifts to Riley. I tap my screen, and it illuminates my dark space. I stare at the device, willing a text from Riley to magically pop up, but it's useless. Riley doesn't speak directly to me anymore. He goes through Tahlia, because for some reason, she's the only person he can somewhat tolerate right now—that half-hunter blood, I suppose. My phone vibrates and a new text from Callen flashes on my screen.

Callen: Stop by The Perk on your way to school. I have a new drink I want you to try. :) I hope you like cinnamon.

Izzy: I suppose I can make time for you when you're offering free coffee.

Callen: Coffee is my love language, Beswick. Now get up or you're going to be late for school!

School, ugh—it's a dread. That whole being alone thing. Thank God it's Friday. It's a shame Callen isn't in high school anymore. It'd be nice to have at least one friend. After Mrs. Jamison's mysterious disappearance, as the town is calling it, our history class has been split up. Even though I'd love to see Riley, I know my life is at risk by doing so, and by the grace of whatever luck I have left, Riley is no longer in my class. That saves a lot of nervous mornings looking over my shoulder, hoping my ex-boyfriend won't rush the room and attack me, putting my coven and all the hunters at risk of being found out. But Tahlia is also no longer in my class. With Riley now a full-blown hunter and her fate lingering in the air, they've grown closer. I can understand why; they're both struggling. I don't blame them, but I'm jealous. I'm jealous that Tahlia is close to Riley, and Riley is closer to Tahlia than I currently am.

Did I really expect things to go back to normal after the forest? No, but I hoped it would bring us all closer, not push us away.

"Izzy." My dad knocks on my door, rocking me from my endless loop of destructive thoughts. "You better be awake."

"I'm up. I'm up," I shout, crossing the room.

Dad's hand is raised when I open the door, ready to knock again. He looks impeccably groomed with his freshly shaven face and crisp white buttoned-up shirt paired with a baby blue tie. I smile. It's nice seeing him healthy and back to his old self.

Dad's eyes crinkle as a concerned grin twitches across his lips. He knows something is off with me, but I haven't been able to tell him a thing. He's been through enough recently. I can't do that to him.

"Sweetie, I'm heading out early. Still playing catch up from missing all that work. I hate skipping breakfast with you. I really miss our mornings together. Things haven't been the same since my stint in the hospital, and then the day hikers . . ." His face turns solemn.

The day hikers finally found Anna's body, I finish his sentence in my head.

Images of her spirit evaporating like mist in the afternoon sun cross over my eyes like it's happening right in front of me all over again. Anna's body was magically returned to precisely where it was supposed to be, and eventually, hikers stumbled upon it as originally planned. However, it was many days later, and her skin had already become unrecognizable from what Tim said. I imagine it was really gross. Of course, my dad left out that part after he identified the body and told me what happened. But I know her soul is safe now and in another realm with her mother—or at least, I hope so. It was one good thing that came from that day, along with breaking the link from Anna incarnate to my dad, which was what was keeping him sick. We did what we set out to do that day. We saved Anna to save my dad.

"Earth to Izzy." Dad snaps his fingers in front of my eyes. "Do I need to worry about you? You space out a lot lately."

I tuck my untamed hair behind my ears. "Um, no. Sorry. I have a lot on my plate. I was thinking about my history test first period."

"OK, sweetie. I hope that's all." His eyes stay fixed on mine, unwavering in his classic concerned dad gaze. "Do you need me to make you any breakfast before I head out?"

"No, I'm stopping by The Perk on my way to school. I'll be fine."

"Please make sure you get something other than just coffee and sugar."

"I will, Dad. Promise."

"You sure have been spending a lot of time with that boy. He's nice. I like him."

"Dad, we're just friends. How many times do I have to tell you that?"

Dad lets out a short, uncomfortable chuckle. His shoulders tense up, and I know he wishes my mom was here for these types of conversations.

"You know you can tell me what happened between you and Riley? I was kind of rooting for you two after I saw you holding hands that day on the street with your friends."

I nervously rock on the heels of my feet. "We were just too different, that's all. Maybe in another life." I grin.

Dad runs his fingers through his dark hair, and the smell of his woodsy shampoo lingers in the air between us. "You know, I kind of miss both those Hawkins men. Tim's been so busy lately. I've hardly seen him since I left the hospital."

That's by design.

"I still have a lot of work that needs to be done before winter. If you see Riley around, tell him I'll pay him if he wants to come over and help. It was so nice having him here with Tim. The kid's pretty strong."

Witch hunter strong.

"I will, but I doubt he'll have time. He's been swamped. I hear that the football team is gearing up for homecoming next weekend, and they've been doing double practices."

"Oh, is that right? Are you planning on going to the homecoming dance, sweetie?"

"I haven't given it much thought."

Lies. It's all I think about.

Although, I thought I would have a date with my boyfriend, Riley, the newly freed hunter. But fate had other plans for us.

Stupid rival coven cursing us before we could undo the hunter's curse.

"Izzy, I swear." Dad snaps his fingers again.

"Sorry, a lot on my mind."

"Clearly." He frowns. "I'm going to take off. I'll see you for dinner tonight, right?"

"Yes, I'll be home."

Shutting the door, I smile, happy to have my dad home and healthy. He has no memory of the events leading up to his poisoning or his time in the hospital. When we told him he ingested hemlock, he truly believed some drifted into his mouth while he was in the forest searching for me and Anna.

Thankfully, my dad didn't need Jonathan Kent's kidney. I still hope to reach out to him, but first, I need to make sure he's a good person. We don't need anyone evil coming into our lives. We've had enough of that to last a lifetime.

***

After a quick shower, I rush to get dressed, as I'm always running late. I toss on a plain, gray, lightweight sweater, push up my sleeves, and shimmy into a pair of faded, slightly frayed jeans. I don't spend much time on my makeup and hair routine because, let's face it, I don't have anyone to impress. Selecting the right pair of shoes takes me some time, but I finally decide on black and white Converse—no more flip-flops for this girl. You never know when you need to scale the side of a cliff. Plus, the weather is changing. The heatwave is over, and I finally get to see the autumn colors on all the trees here. It's just as beautiful as I hoped it'd be, not that I've given myself much time to enjoy it, but it's what I love most about my walk to school, besides the free coffee from Callen, of course.

I sling my backpack on and race down the stairs, checking the clock on my phone—just enough time to swing by The Perk.

My hand is on the door, feeling the smoothness of the handle beneath my fingers, when the sound of a faint rattle from the other side stops me in my tracks. It's so quiet. I pull back to wait for it again. There's a distinct vibration in the air, one I haven't felt since my magic disappeared. My fingers tingle as I reach for the handle once again.

A faint, rhythmic patter gently shakes the door.

Who can this be?

I drag the door back. My eyes rapidly flutter, taking in the sight of the unfamiliar girl standing on my doorstep. Her unruly, honey-brown hair that's in desperate need of a trim stirs up around her face.

"Can I help you?" I inquire timidly, my voice quavering slightly. Everything has me on edge these days.

The girl gazes at me with her large, emerald eyes. "Hi, I'm Scarlet. We need to talk."

CHAPTER 02
SCARLET

The words of the unfamiliar girl stun me in place.

"Excuse me, do I know you?" My response is weighted with curiosity.

She bats her long, un-mascaraed eyelashes. "No, not exactly."

I nod, encouraging her to continue. After all, she's the one who knocked on my door.

The girl clumsily stumbles over her long legs, her nerves getting the better of her. She tugs on her honey-brown hair that's draping down her shoulders.

I gaze at the strange girl, the silence growing louder as I await her reply.

"I'm not sure how to say this, but . . ." she pauses.

My patience is dwindling, yet insatiable curiosity keeps my feet rooted to the ground. A flurry of vibrant red and orange leaves dance in a frenzy around my doorstep, creating a natural barrier between us. I take a step closer; the leaves rustle and crackle beneath my shoes, puncturing the silence between us. She recoils from my approach as if the mere sight of me fills her with fear.

"It's OK. You can tell me. Why are you here?" I coax.

She takes a shy step backward. "It's complicated."

I snicker. "I understand complicated. It's a language I speak well."

She gives me a curious grin as she shifts uncomfortably in her raggedy shoes, leaving them in a pigeon-toe stance. "I've been watching you," she whispers, hunching into herself.

Watching me?

The hairs on the back of my neck stand erect. I'm the one taking a step back this time, the air growing chillier between us.

"Izzy," she says softly, almost inaudibly.

She knows my name.

"Who are you? I question, mimicking her hushed voice.

My eyes shift past her, down the street, wondering if she's alone. Suddenly, my phone vibrates in my hand, causing me to jump. I assume it's Callen, wondering where I am, but I resist the urge to check. Instead, I slip it into my back pocket, keeping my eyes fixed on the stranger in my doorway.

"I know everything," she says, her words laced with accusation.

Impossible.

"Scarlet—if that's even your real name—I think it's time you leave. I don't know what kind of joke you're playing on me, but you need to go," I respond, nervously gulping down my words.

Her wide, oval-shaped eyes scan every inch of my body with sharp scrutiny, as if trying to decipher my thoughts.

I take a cautious step back into the house.

My fingers curl around the handle on the door, ready to push it shut, but her arm shoots out and latches onto mine, gripping me so tight it hurts. Flames wildly dance up my arm, crossing over my chest and up my throat, nearly suffocating me.

I cough, feeling lightheaded and faint. I look the girl straight in the eyes as a tsunami of fire illuminates her emerald gaze.

A witch?

I peel her tightly clenched fingers from my arm. With a shove, I send her stumbling backward through the doorway, slamming the door in her face. An echoing bang reverberates through the foyer, shaking the hall tree mirror.

Gasping for air, I collapse to the floor. As the fire coursing through me slowly fades away, I'm left with a burning sensation where she touched my skin. Her handprint seared me like a red-hot iron.

My hand trembles as I reach into my back pocket for my phone. Two unread messages from Callen illuminate the screen.

Callen: On your way? Margo and T are in the store. Thought you'd like to know.

Callen: I'm getting worried. Where are you?

I type out my response, careful not to alarm him and send him into a save Izzy frenzy.

Izzy: Sorry. I'm on my way. Tell them to wait.

Callen: You want me to have the girls wait? Why?

Izzy: Something crazy just happened.
Callen: Is everything OK?
Izzy: I just felt something I haven't felt in 37 days.
Callen: Get your ass here. NOW!

Callen's right. I need to get to The Perk.

It's important that my *friends* hear what happened. They need to be informed, regardless of the state of our relationship. The urgency to leave my house has my nerves on edge, but the possibility of encountering the girl is even more unsettling.

I hate being so unprotected.

I gingerly run my right hand along the door, feeling for any vibrations or tremors, while gripping my cell phone in my other hand, ready to call for reinforcements if necessary. But nothing happens.

No fire.

No magic.

No connection to the girl that mysteriously showed up on my doorstep.

With utmost stealth, I glance out the door, allowing only a tiny opening to see through. I slip my head through the crack, keeping my hand on the handle, checking both sides before looking down at the street.

She's gone.

I think.

Clutching my phone tightly with Callen's number pulled up, ready to call at a moment's notice, I slip through the thin crack and hastily lock the door behind me.

I descend the stairs, my feet pounding against each

concrete step as I make my way to the street, swiftly crossing to the other side. I check over my shoulder, waiting for the mystery girl to pop out, but she remains elusive.

Who the hell are you, Scarlet?

Even the thought of her name makes my skin burn. I glance down at the imprint of her tiny hand branded into my supple skin, and I'm plagued with more questions.

Could she be part of the rival coven?

CHAPTER 03
DEATH AND DESTRUCTION

Standing outside The Perk, gazing at the good-looking boy behind the counter, expertly slinging coffee, instantly puts me at ease.

For his customers, a fake smile is plastered across his face, but I can tell he's rigid with worry, and with good reason. Our connection isn't necessary to understand why. All my problems always end up on his shoulders. He's taken it upon himself to be my protector, and I'm grateful for his unwavering dedication. I feel better knowing he's always here for me. But does that make me a bad person for allowing him to take on my issues as his own?

My stomach rolls as I pull the door open, dreading what's awaiting me on the other side. Can I really face Tahlia and Margo after everything we've been through? Trouble always finds me, and this is just another example of that. Why couldn't this strange girl have ended up on their doorstep instead?

The entire coffee shop hums with conversation when I step inside, but it all becomes background static when

Callen's dark gaze meets mine. His face relaxes, and a hint of a smile appears. It's just me and him, and for the briefest of moments, I feel like everything will be OK.

"About time, Beswick." Callen unties his black apron and swings it over his shoulder. "I'm taking my break," he hollers to his co-worker at the register.

I flash him a grin, but I know it's tinged with unease.

Callen slides a large, iced beverage with a mound of cinnamon clinging to the lid across the counter. He gives a slight nod to the girls sitting at a French-style café table for two in the rear of the store. "Meet you in just a second." He disappears around the corner.

I want to run over to the girls and spill everything, but I don't. We don't have that kind of relationship anymore. Instead, I take out my phone and mindlessly flip through my photo gallery while I wait for Callen. I haven't taken many photos since I moved here. Most of my gallery is filled with Sondra, Evelyn, and Mackenzie. The sight of them makes me shudder, but I can't help but wonder how Evelyn and Mackenzie are doing. If I didn't delete all of my socials, maybe I would know, but it's probably better this way. What I don't know can't hurt me, right? *Always the fool.*

"So, what the hell happened?" Callen asks, startling me, nudging his shoulder against mine.

"I want to tell everyone at once. To be honest, I'm still trying to process it all." I take a large sip of my beverage, swallowing a little too much cinnamon for my preference.

Callen's face fills with a mixture of emotions. His lips press into a thin line that conveys both distress and curiosity.

"OK, are you sure you want to get them involved?"

"No, but it would be reckless if I didn't tell them."

"Now I'm dying to know. You're really worrying me, Beswick."

I frown, taking a step toward the girls. Callen's hand wraps around my arm, tugging me back.

"You know I always support you. Always. But keep in mind how fragile Margo is right now."

My frown deepens, practically drooping down to my chin. "Don't you think I always have her in mind? I hate that I ruined things between us. I miss her so much that it feels like a part of me is dead."

"OK. I trust you know what you're doing. Into the lion's den we go."

For some reason, rage is now boiling under my skin. I thought I'd be nervous to talk to the girls again, but instead, I'm angry.

It shouldn't be like this.

I've been robbed, not only of my magic, but my happiness. The rival coven cursed my life—put a big fat hex on everything good I had. I'm at war with a coven that is no longer on this earth, and that ignites a fury within me that makes my skin burn—and not with the good fire that should be coursing through me.

One look at the girls, and my body turns to ice.

My heart pounds in my chest so loudly I swear Callen hears it, because he turns to me and mouths, "You got this." He reaches for my free hand and squeezes it once before letting it drop.

It's strange not having our connection, yet butterflies zip through my stomach at his touch. *Could there really be more here?*

Sitting with their backs facing us, the girls are chatting and laughing. I hate to take this moment of happiness away from them.

Here comes Izzy, the bearer of bad news.

As always, Tahlia's hair is a striking sight, with a wild mass of black curls tamed into an intentionally messy yet perfect bun atop her gorgeous head. Her posture is impeccable, with her back straight and shoulders squared, giving off an air of confidence and poise that makes her seem unapproachable, while Margo's relaxed slouch is the complete opposite.

Margo exudes a peaceful and carefree aura, even after everything she's been through. Her luscious locks, a beautiful blend of red and brown, flow down her back in a mesmerizing cascade, taking me away from the dreadful moment I'm about to walk into.

I miss them so much.

The sound of my shoes intrusively skidding against the floor gives away our presence.

Margo's head turns slowly. Her frigid gaze meets mine briefly before she turns back to the table and leans in to whisper something to Tahlia. Her long hair swishes across the back of her chair before settling into place.

Despite being practically on top of them now, both girls refuse to turn around and face us. Callen clears his throat, making our presence undeniable.

"You guys can't hate me forever," I say, keeping my voice low, afraid I'll break into tears if I raise it the slightest.

"Watch me," Margo hisses.

I miss the old Margo.

"Come on, girls. We need to stick together," I plead.

"You lied to me," Margo responds, pain stacked in her voice.

"We all lied to you. I know that doesn't make it better," I add.

Both girls twist in their seats, their knees touching, giving Callen and me only a partial view of their faces.

"But you were the one who knew the truth," Margo says, seething. "Tahlia and Jessa really thought they hit a deer, especially after *you* framed Sam Hornsby for Megan's death"—she glares at Callen—"that was their truth because you made it their truth."

Sam Hornsby.

The mention of his name sets off a jarring alarm in my gut. I had no control over what Callen did to protect us, but I still feel bad about it.

"That's right. Callen told us the truth," Tahlia chimes in.

I already knew that, but it feels like a jab at me. After the day in the forest, he had no choice but to tell them the truth.

"What about Jessa? She's the one who did it." The words slip from my mouth. After all this time trying to protect her, I so freely toss her under the Jeep, so to speak, to make myself seem less at fault.

"Do you see her sitting here with us?" Margo asks.

"Well, no." I pause. "I'm sorry, Margo. I really am. I thought I was protecting you. I didn't want to believe that Jessa really ran over Megan. That would mean our friend could go to jail, and what Callen did to cover it up could have exposed us all. I thought I was keeping our coven safe. We fucked up. Tahlia and I should have made Jessa stop that night."

Tahlia glares at me.

If looks could kill.

"I'm so sorry. I wish I could go back to that night and change things, but I can't." My eyes drop to the ground as shame fills me from my feet up.

Silence permeates the air, and time seems to stop, leaving us lingering on the truth.

Margo huffs, filling the space back up with her annoyance at my presence. "So, tell me, why are we"—she whips her finger in the distance between her and Tahlia—"still here? What happened to you now?"

Ouch. Harsh.

I take a deep breath and flash my arm between the two girls. "I had a visitor this morning."

Callen grabs my arm, bringing it closer to his eyes. "What the—" he shouts. "Who hurt you?" he questions, lowering his voice as a couple of customers turn their attention to us.

"I honestly don't know who she is. She could be a part of the rival coven for all I know. I'm not sure. She knocked on my door, introducing herself only as Scarlet. But she couldn't explain who she was. She said she's been watching me and knows everything. Then she hurt me." I shake my arm as a visual reminder. "So, I don't know what to think. She was gangly looking, with long honey-brown hair, green eyes, very plain and dressed poorly."

Gosh, I sound like Sondra.

"Does she sound familiar?" I ask.

Both girls shake their heads, and Callen shrugs his shoulders.

"What should we do about her?" I ask.

"This sounds like an Izzy problem. Count me out," Margo says, standing. "I can't get involved this time. Come on, T. We're going to be late."

T.

Margo gets to call her T.

Things are changing. She sounds like Jessa.

Is Margo the new Jessa?

"You need to listen to me. I think she's a witch. I felt my fire when she grabbed me. It was as if her touch uncorked something inside of me. I don't know who she is, but feeling that again—my fire—gave me a glimmer of hope. Maybe we can get our magic back and fix everything—the hunter's curse and the rival coven's curse—all of it."

"Can you fix all of the death and destruction?" Margo asks, almost mockingly. "Every time we get involved with you, someone dies." She swings her backpack over her shoulder.

"Margo. Wait," I call out.

"Like I said, count me out. I don't think it's the curses. I think it's you—you're the curse. We were fine before you showed up."

Ouch.

A vast change since the last time we were here together. Memories of us sitting on the green love seat behind me, back when we were solid, zip through my mind.

"Are you serious? That really hurts. I thought we were like sisters."

"Sisters?" Margo laughs. "Sisters take care of each other. They don't lie to each other." She reaches for the black and purple pendant necklace that used to hang across her chest, but it's no longer there, so she runs her fingers over her collarbone instead.

Tears fill my eyes. I try not to blink for fear of them falling uncontrollably. I hate showing signs of weakness. Mean girls use it against you. I never wanted to think that of Margo, but she's acting like a mean girl right now. But I did that to her, so maybe I'm the mean girl—the bully—the Sondra.

I shake the thought from my head. We aren't like that—well, maybe Jessa is sometimes. For the most part, I believe we're good people who make mistakes—except for Margo. Her only mistake is falling blindly into a friendship with me.

"I just thought we could try to figure it out as a group—a coven."

"There is no coven anymore. You broke us."

Tears sting my eyes.

Margo's shoulder hits mine as she hurriedly brushes past us, leaving me with my mouth hanging open in disbelief. Tahlia trails behind her without a word.

"What did I expect?" I say under my breath.

"You expected your friends to be there for you. I'll talk to my sister," Callen responds.

How did I get so lucky to find a friend like Callen? He's the one constant in my life. I need to nurture this friendship, or I'll lose it too.

My eyes dart to the clock on the wall. "I have to get going.

I have about point five seconds before I'm tardy."

"I have to get back to work too. As always, I have my phone on me if you need anything. If that girl shows up again, call me immediately. Things were so much easier when we were connected."

The pain of our dissolved connection cuts through his inky black eyes. "I'll pick you up after school, and we can discuss this mystery girl scenario in more detail. We'll figure out who she is and what she wants with you."

The smell of freshly brewed coffee fills the air as I follow Callen through the narrow walkway of eclectic chairs, tables, and couches. Callen abruptly stops in his tracks, making me stumble into him. My free hand involuntarily wraps around his waist for support, and his washboard abs pleasantly greet me through his black shirt.

"Is that Riley?" Callen asks.

Without removing my hand, I poke my head around him and follow his line of sight to the street. Riley's sitting in his car, staring intensely into the coffee shop. Even at a distance, I can make out every feature on his face. His sculpted jaw is tight and clenched. His sandy brown hair is falling over his forehead in a tussled, attractive mess. I wish I could reach out and push it back, to catch a glimpse of his brilliant blue eyes. But then I remember his eyes are no longer the blue I fell in love with. They're now tainted with his hunter blood, swirling with colors that don't belong to him.

Different shades of emotions flash through me.

Love. Hate. Desire. Anger. All of them taking up residence in my heart.

Callen's protective energy radiates from him; his muscles tense, and his glower is unrelenting. He glances down at my hand wrapped around his midsection, and I let it drop, as does my stomach from the intense feeling it stirred inside me.

I'm more conflicted than I realized.

This might be a problem.

When Riley eyes us, he white-knuckles the steering wheel and pulls into traffic without looking, nearly sideswiping a passing car. Both vehicles lay on their horn, then Riley speeds away.

"What the hell? Was he watching us?" I ask.

"Who knows with lover boy? He's a complicated mess."

"It's not his fault."

"I know." Callen hangs his head and turns to head back to his shift. "See you later, Beswick. Be smart. Don't do anything stupid today. And please stay away from Riley."

Part of me wants to disobey Callen's request and chase after Riley, but I know I shouldn't. He could kill me.

Another piece of me—an undeniable piece I didn't know existed until now, wants to jump over the counter and kiss Callen.

I'm the complicated mess.

CHAPTER 04
ANOTHER IZZY PROBLEM

The first-period bell pierces through the air, abruptly ending the lively chatter in the hallway. On cue, the students disperse, disappearing behind closed doors. I grab my books, feeling a rush of anxiety as I slam my locker shut.

Late again.

Without wasting another moment, I take off down the A-wing hallway, my Converse shoes squeaking against the freshly polished floor, leaving behind faint black skid marks as I go.

Sorry, Janitor Jim.

At the end of the hallway, room 103's door is closing.

Mr. Pearson, my new teacher, has a rule that once the door closes, you're late. If I had my magic, I bet I could keep it open long enough to slink inside. I increase my speed, but the door shuts without me on the inside.

Dang it!

I can't do anything right—can't even make it to school on time.

My self-deprecation turns to fear as my eyes focus on a

hooded figure standing unnaturally against the wall on the opposite side of my classroom. Their gaunt-looking frame is nearly pressed flush against the wall.

Scarlet?

Did she follow me to school?

She can't hurt me here, right?

"Did you follow me?" I ask, taking a cautious step closer.

The figure's head twists, and a wild mess of jet-black hair tumbles from the hood.

Not Scarlet.

I gasp. "Sam Hornsby?"

His sad, dark eyes greet mine.

"How are you here?" I question, realizing how rude I sound after it's too late to reel the words back in.

His shoulders slouch forward, and he slowly pivots in my direction. He looks awful. His hollowed eyes are pronounced against his high cheekbones, and his skin is ashen and dull-looking. Did they not feed him in lock-up?

I take a slow step back.

"Izzy, right?"

I nod. "You're out of jail? But I thought—"

"Innocent until proven guilty, right?" He nervously laughs. "Turns out they can't find me guilty. The evidence against me was tampered with, or something is now missing." He shrugs his shoulders. "The whole case was a fucking joke if you ask me."

Oh my gosh. Callen's spell must have worn off when our magic was taken away. How did we not think of that? Guilt flashes like a blinking light across all of my features.

Smile, Izzy. Sam can't think you're hiding something.

"My lawyer said there is no case now, and they let me go yesterday." He kicks at the floor, avoiding eye contact.

How did we not hear this?

"They're still trying to get me on drug charges, but my lawyer said I'll probably just get community service, since I had time served already or something like that—if they even still have a case. I don't get any of this stuff. At least I'm not going away for something I didn't do."

"So, you didn't have anything to do with Megan's death?" I ask the question he's waiting for, even though I know the answer. It'd be weird if I didn't ask.

"You were there that night. I was talking to you. I was drunk, but I remember everything."

"Yes, that's right. We spoke." I offer him a flat smile.

Sam's lips purse, and his eyes narrow. He leans closer to me, like he wants to tell me a secret. "You know, I didn't even get a chance to talk to her that night. She was my friend. I didn't want to sleep with her like everyone is saying. Plus, she once told me in secrecy that she likes girls. So, why would I bother? I shouldn't be spilling her secrets like this, but whatever. What's done is done."

His eyes grow misty as he fights back tears. "I would never have done that to her. Please, you have to believe me and tell your friends. Help me spread the word of my innocence."

"Sure, I believe you."

Sam offers me a glint of a smile.

"Are you back in school?"

He parts his lips, but the door to my classroom swings

open. Mr. Pearson frowns at me, leaving the door ajar.

"Mr. Hornsby, here are your home-school assignments for my class." He pushes a pile of paperwork into Sam's hands. "Please return them all by the end of the week. Now, go check in with the rest of your teachers, and leave the premises quickly. Next time, send your father. The students are in an uproar that you're even here."

"But he's not guilty," I say, defending Sam.

"Miss Beswick, inside now, or I'll hand you a tardy slip."

Sam mouths the words, "Thank you."

It's the least I can do. You know, that whole 'I feel bad for framing you for murder' thing.

Nodding to Sam, I keenly maneuver around my teacher and into my classroom. My heart's racing.

Inside the room, I exhale sharply, feeling a slight sense of relief, but also hyperaware that Sam's release could cause problems for us. At least he doesn't have to spend a life behind bars because of us. So, there's that.

My eyes fall on Margo, desperate to make eye contact with her, but our meeting falls short, and Mr. Pearson returns.

I quickly type out a group message, including Tahlia, Margo, Jessa, and Callen, as I pretend to search my backpack for my book.

Izzy: WE NEED TO TALK! I just saw Sam in the hallway. He's out of jail.

Three green dots flicker across the bottom of the screen.

Margo's typing . . .

Callen: I just heard the news.

I stare at my screen, waiting for Margo to type something—anything—but the little green dots vanish. I twist in my seat to face Margo. Her expression is inscrutable, like a statue carved from stone.

Please, look at me!

Something needs to resonate with the girls. If mystery witch girl isn't enough reason to talk, Sam Hornsby is. We need to be on the same page to keep Jessa safe, if that's even what Margo wants. But I get the feeling this is also an *Izzy problem* with a heaping side of Callen.

CHAPTER 05
SITTING DUCKS

The girls didn't have a change of heart.

There were no text messages or notes—nothing. I was invisible to Margo and Tahlia the rest of the day.

Jessa was a no-show—probably called out sick when she heard the news about Sam. I thought she'd be the first to respond. But nothing—crickets.

From the moment I woke up, everything's gone wrong. Thank goodness school's over, and I'm free from this teenage prison. All my thoughts and emotions are begging to be released and shared with someone. And my someone right now is Callen Latham-Hart. He's the only one who understands me.

My sulky pout instantly turns into a smile at the sight of Callen's freshly washed, sleek, darker-than-night Cadillac. A sigh of relief escapes my mouth as he pulls up and shifts his car into park. I wave and sprint down the steps.

Despite all the uncertainty and turmoil in my life, being with Callen is like finding a calm haven in the midst of a storm. He always has my back, and I enjoy the ease of being around him.

Gosh, is that love?

The sheer thought makes my stomach churn with nervous energy. If only I could release the guilt pulling me into the depths of my sorrow. Riley and I never had time to see our feelings through. He's a hunter, and I'm a powerless witch. Unless something big changes, we can never be together. He left no room for doubt about his feelings for me. We aren't like Bree and Barrett. However, if I can break him from the curse that holds his emotions hostage, we can be together, and I have to have hope. Or I have nothing.

So, where does that leave my heart?

"Hey there, Beswick. We have a lot to talk about."

"Right! Sam Hornsby, what the—" I sling my backpack into the space behind my seat. "I thought mystery witch girl would be our only problem today. Seriously, eff my luck."

He pulls in a deep breath and rests his hand on my arm. A surge of sensations rushes through me, making my insides tingle. "It's going to be OK."

"Um, how exactly is it going to be OK? Are you living in the same world as me? Jessa ran over Megan, and it seems all evidence has returned to its original state. Megan was hit by a car—no drugs were in her system when she actually died. How the hell are they going to explain this, and who will they pin for it now? They're going to find out, Callen. We'll all go to jail, and no one cares but me."

"Calm down, Beswick. I need you to take deep breaths with me."

"Can you please just drive?" I plead, sensing the need to get away from the school as quickly as possible, or I might explode.

Removing his hand from my arm, he takes the wheel and sharply turns away from the school, pulling into the flow of traffic. "Megan was cremated last month. There's no way to exhume and test a body that no longer exists. It's over, Izzy."

"Sh-she was cremated?" I stutter.

"Yes, that's what I read in the newspaper right before I came to pick you up. No one will ever know you girls had anything to do with Megan's death. Don't worry; I already smoothed things over via text with my sister. Discreetly, of course. It's Jessa we need to worry about. Did you see her today?"

"No, she wasn't at lunch or our two classes afterward. I figured she heard the news and faked sick. She's probably somewhere freaking out. Her denial story that she's been telling herself isn't adding up anymore."

"We'll keep an eye on her. She can only hurt herself. If she tosses us under the bus, she'd be admitting fault first. The murder came before the cover-up. Plus, who'd believe that a modern-day coven of witches covered up a hit and run." He chuckles.

"A witch hunt can start anywhere, Callen. History tends to repeat itself, and this day and age, anything is possible."

"Just please don't worry about it. Plus, her dad's running for mayor, remember? This would be the worst time for something like this to get out. She needs to keep a low profile and play the doting daughter."

I squirm restlessly in my seat. "Where is the four-wheeled murder weapon, anyway?"

Callen sighs. "It's still best that you don't know. But it's somewhere it won't be found."

"How can you be so sure?" I bite at my bottom lip.

"Izzy, do you trust me?"

I hesitate for a moment and notice the disappointment in his expression. I twist my body to face him more directly. He's holding his breath, waiting for my response.

I reach out and let my hand rest atop his on the steering wheel. "Callen, you're the only person I trust as of lately. Well, besides my dad."

He lets out a long breath, and a smirk of satisfaction spreads across his face.

I pull my hand back, and he lets his drop to his leg, palm upward almost as an invitation to lace my fingers between his. *Tempting.*

But now's not the time to overthink our relationship, friendship, confusing-ship—whatever-kind-of ship this is, so I clear my throat, diverting the tension inside the car back to our issue at hand. "So, onto our next problem on the agenda. What do we do about the mystery witch girl?"

In a low voice, he says, "We stay vigilant. Since we know nothing about her, we really can't do anything until she comes out again."

"Sitting ducks," I respond.

"Pretty much." Callen's eyes diligently check every direction, including a double take in the review mirror. "I wasn't there this morning, and I didn't experience what you did, so I have to ask, do you really think she's one of them— part of the rival coven?"

The thought of them sends shivers down my spine, and their spell circles in my head as if on command, reminding me of the loss of my magic. "Maybe," I softly reply.

Callen scrunches his nose and purses his lips into a flat line.

"You don't think she's one of them, do you?" I ask.

He strokes his chin before returning his hand to the steering wheel. "What I can't stop thinking about is that she came to you. Maybe she's not evil."

"Of course, she's evil!" I shout.

"Here me out." He waggles his finger at me, keeping his eyes on the road. "If she were one of them, don't you think it would have been a surprise attack? Or worse, like some kind of revenge assault for killing her coven mates?"

"Hello!" I hastily pull up my sleeve. "She hurt me, remember?" My arm shoots across the center console, hovering inches from his chest, asserting my point, making my injury hard to refute.

Confusion clouds his face as lines of puzzlement etch deep into his features. "It's healing. It's almost gone," he says.

"Huh?" With doubt, I pull my arm into my focus and examine it intently. He's right; it's nearly healed.

"That's so strange," I mutter, unable to take my eyes off my arm. "I really thought I'd be scarred for life."

"Maybe it was her way of communicating with you— showing you she's like you," Callen suggests.

"Was like me." I pout, crossing my arms tightly under my chest.

The corners of his mouth turn downward. "You know you're not the only one who lost their magic that day?"

Like a hefty anchor of guilt, my head drops into my hands. "I'm sorry. I didn't mean to imply—"

The car comes to a halt, breaking me from my sentence, and I jerk my head up. I hadn't realized we were at my house already.

"I know, Izzy. This whole thing has messed us all up."

I twist in my seat, locking eyes with him, and we exchange a knowing look of forgiveness—a silent agreement that the past is already behind us. That's what I love about our friendship, even without our shared connection, we still understand each other.

But in case I'm wrong, I swiftly divert the conversation to another topic. "So, have you heard anything new with the necklaces? Please tell me the adults are closer to figuring out what the rival coven was using them for besides to spy on us? There has to be more to them."

He shakes his head. "You ask every day, and the answer is the same."

"I think they should give us a chance with them," I say with determination in my voice.

Callen crinkles his brow. "Not happening. They don't want us getting into any more trouble, and can you blame them?"

"I suppose not, but we're the ones who cracked the bloodline curse. I know if I can get my hands on them, I can figure it out." I curl both of my hands out in front of me.

With a lifted brow, he asks, "We didn't break the hunter's curse, so what makes you think you can figure this mystery out?"

"Well, I'm sure I would've broken the hunter's curse if the rival coven didn't steal my magic. So, not my fault." I flick my hair over my shoulder in a somewhat cocky manner.

"Don't you remember what Isobel said? All the hunters must die, or all the bloodline witches must die for the curse to be broken. We were never going to break it, Izzy." Callen sighs.

I raise my index finger and shake it in his face. "Nope. I don't take that as an answer. I know if I could touch the necklaces—hold them in my hand—I could figure it out."

"Izzy, I haven't even seen the necklaces since that day in the forest. My parents have them under lock and key somewhere."

"Ugh! This is so frustrating." I rock back in my seat.

Callen thoughtfully tilts his head to the side. "I'm not saying it's not. I understand your frustration, but we're dealing with spells and curses dating back centuries. Whatever happens, it's not going to be an easy road."

"I know." My lips form a full pout.

I reach to unlatch my seatbelt, but then I hesitate and pull back. "I'm not ready to go home yet," I say.

Callen doesn't waste any time and pulls back onto Jefferson Place.

I roll down my window, and the wind tousles my hair, bringing the refreshing October air with it. "I wish there were somewhere we could go. You know, to get away from all this chaos."

"I think I know just the place."

CHAPTER 06
JUST RELAX

Callen to the rescue again, but this time, I asked for it.

"So, where exactly are you whisking me away to that escapes all the madness in my life?" I ask with a dramatic backhand across my forehead, giving my best damsel in distress act, and failing miserably at it.

"Eh, eh—hush." He shakes his finger at me. "Now, don't go worrying yourself with that little lady. Just sit back and enjoy the ride," he says, playing into my theatrics.

I flash him a grateful smile.

"But do me a favor, please?"

I raise my brow.

"Try to relax—just this one time. Then you can return to being the worried and stressed Izzy I know so well. I know that's a big ask, and it's hard for you to do." He laughs.

I slump in my seat, trying to imitate my best relaxed look. "Hey, I can relax."

"Prove it."

"I am. See, look at me—all chillaxed." I drop my shoulders even further and let my features droop.

"I didn't say look like an ogre."

"An ogre!" I attempt to stifle my laugh, but a huff of a chuckle manages to escape, turning into uncontrollable laughter.

"There she is, the fun Izzy. Every once in a while, I get to see a glimmer of her." A smile lights up his face.

"Yup. If it's fun Izzy you want, then a fun, relaxed Izzy you will get."

"Perfect. It's all I've ever wanted."

Callen rolls down the remaining windows. I extend my hand and let the cool wind pass through my fingers. He veers right onto Winchester Avenue, where the road winds up the picturesque bluff of colorful maple, oak, and elm trees.

He slows the car, pulls over to the side of the road and gestures for me to step out and join him. I take my time getting out of the vehicle as there is a steep drop-off outside my door. One wrong step, and it's goodbye Izzy. Good thing I'm not wearing my flip-flops.

We make ourselves comfortable by posting up side by side against the warm hood of his freshly washed SUV.

"Wow. I've never been up here before. It's absolutely breathtaking." I flash him an approving grin.

The town of East Gate could be straight out of a magazine, with the fall foliage as a backdrop to all the historic buildings.

"You've been too preoccupied with things outside your control to take in everything East Gate has to offer."

"Hey, I used to have fun with Tim and my dad before I knew Tim was a murdering psycho that an ancient witch cursed in an attempt to destroy my family."

Callen frowns.

"But I know what you mean. Since the moment I walked into Gran-gran's house, I've been consumed and plagued with curses and death. I've allowed zero time for fun and relaxing."

"Seriously, Izzy. Just look at this place. I've lived here my whole life, and this view never gets old. There's something calming and peaceful about it."

I take a moment and allow myself to fully see my newish home of East Gate. It's like I'm seeing it for the first time. The fire-colored autumn leaves blaze down the hillside and back up the valley, with white church steeples standing out like beacons amidst the backdrop. But instead of feeling at peace like Callen, an unsettling feeling flushes through me, giving me goosebumps.

I furrow my brows, and I know lines are forming across my forehead, giving away my thoughts. Callen catches my unsettled giveaway and raises his eyebrow to match mine.

"Sorry, I know I'm supposed to be taking in all this beauty. I know you brought me here to relax. But—"

"But, what? Come on, spit it out, Beswick."

I huff. "But I can't help but wonder why our ancestors chose to settle here." The words fly out of my mouth.

Callen gives me a questioning grin.

"Religion and witches always seem to find each other—like a flame to a moth. Weren't some of these churches once Puritan churches?" I ask.

"I guess so. I know some Puritans ended up here."

"Exactly."

"But none of these churches are practicing that religion anymore," he responds.

I scrunch my nose. "I figured that much, but Lydia and Dinah could have started over anywhere at any time, but they chose a place similar to where they came from. They waited in their purgatory just to come back and be around the same type of people who accused them a century earlier of being witches. I know the town was new when they settled here, but the people around them carried similar values as the exact place they escaped from. Well, except for that whole 'let's hunt and kill witches' thing that the Puritans supposedly stopped doing in 1693. Little did everyone know that others were tasked with that, who, I might add, also settled in this town—the hunters."

"Remember that whole 'let's relax' thing you were going to try?" Callen asks. "But I get what you're saying."

"Sorry, I just have so many questions. Everything I do or see lately seems to add more to the list of unknowns. Our family's history is so fucked up."

Callen chuckles. "You can say that again."

"It's like there always has to be a war. Nothing can exist as is," I add.

"Right."

"It's like us. Couldn't we have existed as a bunch of teenage witches—blissfully unaware of the bloodline curse, the hunter's curse, and no stupid rival coven cursing us? Just friends existing and learning to harness and play with our magic. We should be playing with Ouija Boards and attempting light as a feather and having fun with our glamour power."

"Yeah, that does sound better."

"Hey, since I'm clearly not going to chill and relax, I have another question for you?"

"Shoot."

"Do you think we'll burn up upon entry if we walk into one of those churches below?"

"Dang, Izzy. That's dark."

"It's a valid question."

"I don't know. I can't say. I've never been to church before."

"Me either. Obviously, my dad wasn't raised in a church with a well-attuned bloodline witch as a grandma and a non-practicing witch as a mother. They would never have stepped foot in a church. And I don't think my mom was part of any organized religion, either. So, I don't think I've ever been inside a church."

"There's only one way to find out. We send Tahlia in to check."

My eyes go wide, and my mouth falls open.

"Dude, I'm kidding. I would never risk my sister's life."

"I know that," I respond, kicking at the ground.

"I shouldn't joke like that. I feel bad that I even said that." He rubs his forehead and shifts on his feet. His features noticeably change.

"Hey, Callen, what's going on?"

"I really hate to say this, but I think Tahlia is changing. With our magic being gone, there isn't much stopping her body from gravitating to the hunter's side."

"What? No. She's not," I say the words, trying to convince myself that he's wrong.

"She's turning colder. Darker. Angrier. I used to think she was going to be a witch, like me, but lately, she's giving off hunter vibes. Her birthday is right around the corner, and there's nothing we can do. Whenever you bring up us trying to fix the problem, I'm reminded that her time is limited. I can't talk to my parents, especially my mom, because she's a hunter. She won't understand where I'm coming from, and I don't want to offend her. I'm sure she'd rather have Tahlia become like her, so she's not alone in our family."

What, so they can have cage time together?

"I'm so sorry, Callen. I had no idea you've been so torn up inside. You know you can always confide in me." I rub his shoulder, feeling awful for always making everything about me when my friend's been hurting so much.

I'm an awful friend—to everyone I know.

Callen drops his head and takes a deep breath. When he brings his head back up, he says, "No. This isn't how things are supposed to go. We're going to forget all our problems, even if just for an hour. This spot was a fail, but I'm going to try again. I need this as much as you do."

OK, I promise I'll try to be better.

I quickly text my dad, informing him I'll miss dinner tonight. I feel bad missing time with my dad, but I need to make things right with Callen. I owe him.

My phone vibrates almost immediately.

Dang, Dad, that was fast.

I glance down, but it's not my dad's name I see.

It's Riley's.

CHAPTER 07
MRS. MAPLES

Overwhelming emotions takes over my entire body, making my heart pound and my hands tremble.

Riley's texting me.

After radio silence for weeks, he's finally reaching out.

"Is everything good?" Callen asks, his dark eyes filling with concern.

"Yes," I respond, slipping my phone into my back pocket.

Good thing you can't read my thoughts right now.

Every ounce of me wants to check Riley's text, but I just committed to a no-problem evening with Callen after letting him down. With Riley, I know there will be a problem.

I owe this to my friend.

But Riley.

My heart yanks in two directions yet again.

I muster a smile for Callen. "Let's do this."

"Take two of our relaxed evening is starting in three— two—one," he says, looking at his watch. "All right, Beswick, are you ready for Mrs. Maples?"

"Huh?"

"It's best I don't try to describe it. You need to see Mrs. Maples for yourself to understand its charm."

"Well, I guess you better take me to Mrs. Maples, whatever the heck that is." I laugh and get into the car with my phone burning a hole in my pocket.

After a windy scenic drive back down the picturesque bluff, we pull up to a cute little brown house set back and nestled amongst two taller buildings. A homemade wooden sign hangs above the porch.

Welcome to Mrs. Maples

Open Fall-Winter

"So, this is Mrs. Maples?" I ask, meeting Callen on the sidewalk, staring forward at the old house.

"Yup. You can't live in East Gate, Connecticut without trying some of Mrs. Maples' homemade apple cider."

"Cider, huh? Never pegged you as an apple cider kind of guy."

"Be careful mocking me, or I'll take you apple picking next."

"People really do that?" I question as we follow an uneven sidewalk toward the front door.

He turns to me, his face breaking into a boyish grin that illuminates his dark eyes. "Oh, you bet they do. Fall is a big thing around here, and the leaves are at the height of the season. Our town is about to get invaded by tourists."

"Seriously?"

"Oh, Beswick, you have no idea." He laughs, taking the wooden porch steps two at a time.

On the porch, an elderly woman with an oversized dress and house shoes with uneven socks is pouring cups of hot apple cider from several percolators that are lined up behind her. A folding table is set up with her cash till and hundreds of cups stacked neatly to one side.

"Very quaint," I whisper to Callen.

We get in a small line behind a group of women, all with the same book in their hand. I bet they're in a book club. I try to catch a glimpse of the book's title, but the ladies move forward. I can't remember the last book I read for fun.

When we get closer, I spot a sign taped to her table that simply says *Five Dollars*. It looks like a child wrote it. I suppose it adds to its quaintness.

"Two, please," Callen says when it's our turn.

The woman nods, grabs two cups, and twists her back to pour the drinks. As she turns around, she puffs at a long piece of gray hair that's fallen across her face. She slides the cups across the table as Callen reaches into his wallet for a ten-dollar bill. She grabs it and stuffs the cash in a half-closed till; money's overflowing from it. She must do pretty well for herself.

"Aren't you two just the cutest couple?" the woman says with a sly smirk, finally tucking the fallen hair behind her ear.

"Oh, we're not a couple," I quickly respond.

"Pretty sure I know a couple when I see it. Love is always in the air at Mrs. Maples." She winks at me.

Callen grins.

The wind picks up, sending a cold rush of air sweeping through the trees around the porch.

I shiver, rubbing my hand up and down my sweater.

"Go on, dear. Give her your jacket," Mrs. Maples directs.

"Oh, no. I'm fine." I try to wave him off, but it's too late.

Callen's already taking off his black lapel neck zip-up jacket. He gently hangs it over my shoulders as Mrs. Maples suggested, or more like ordered him to do.

Heat flashes through my cheeks. I imagine I'm turning bright red.

Feeling uncomfortable, I flash both of them an awkward smile as I reach for my cup.

"Thank you," I say to Callen, tilting my drink in his direction, but avoiding looking him straight on.

"Have a good night, dears." Mrs. Maples grins broadly, her eyes shining with happiness. She hums a sweet tune as we walk away.

I wait until we're on the sidewalk before trying to hand Callen his jacket back.

"Oh, no. Keep it on, you're cold."

"The breeze passed. I'm fine now, really." I push the jacket into his hand. "Well, Mrs. Maples is something else, isn't she?"

Callen hands me his drink and slips his coat back on. "She sure is."

You're not picking up on my sarcasm, are you, Callen?

"Tahlia and I would beg our parents to stop here every night leading up to Halloween. They usually caved. We were a dynamic duo. Being only eleven months apart in age, we were in sync with each other on pretty much everything. Our parents were putty in our hands when we teamed up." He grabs his drink from my hand, letting his fingers touch mine.

"That's sweet." I blow at the steam rising from my cup,

watching it disappear into thin air like magic.

"Well, that is, until Tahlia and I started to go our separate ways. We used to be so close until we became teenagers, then we were always at each other's throats."

"Do you think you didn't get along because of your hunter and witch sides unknowingly fighting for dominance?"

He shrugs his shoulders. "Nah, I think it's just what siblings do."

"I wouldn't know," I respond.

"I bet being an only child has its perks."

"Sometimes. But it does get lonely. That's why I was so excited to finally have a group of friends. When Margo said we were like sisters, that really meant something to me."

"Speaking of your *friends*." Callen points across the street.

Jessa is tucking her signature platinum blonde hair inside a white knit hat standing next to her new red Jeep.

"Jessa," I holler, waving in her direction.

Her lips purse and then wrinkle as she shifts her gaze to the bustling sidewalk.

I open my mouth but hesitate as two older individuals join her on the walkway.

"Her parents?" I ask.

"Yup." Callen nods.

Jessa's dad crosses the street first, nearly heading straight at us. He's a tall, athletic looking man with strikingly blond hair and stern features. He is exactly as I pictured him. Inadvertently, I make eye contact with him, causing a moment of awkwardness. His stony gaze lingers on me, making me uneasy.

Callen whispers, "It's not like we can talk to her now anyway with her parents in earshot, plus her dad's not someone you'd want to meet."

Got that right.

"My head drops. What happened to us?"

"I'm sorry, Izzy."

"It's OK." I sniffle, forcing a smile across my face, quickening my pace to avoid running into the Dewitt family.

"Tonight isn't about our problems, remember." I playfully slug him in the shoulder.

He winces and gives me the 'we've talked about the slugging' look.

All I can do is grin. This is one battle he's never going to win.

When we arrive at the car, I'm ready to step toward it, but Callen takes a right, cutting me off, and continues past the SUV. He keeps a slow pace as we stroll down First Avenue toward downtown. I don't question his plans; I welcome them. But my eagerness to embrace his relaxed evening is tempered by the persistent distraction of the unread text message from Riley. I'm dying to see what he has to say after all this time.

"So, where are we going next?" I ask.

"I thought we could walk down Main Street. I know this is your route to school, but it's prettier this time of day. It's the golden hour, right before the sun sets. It's truly something to see in the fall."

"That sounds wonderful."

And awfully romantic.

"What do you think of the cider?"

The steam rising from my cup stings my lips as I try to take a sip. I blow on it again, and the scent of apple, cinnamon, and brown sugar fills the air around me, bringing a sense of welcomed comfort. I take a deep inhale, letting the spices invade my nose once more.

"Eh—still too hot for me, but it smells delightful," I respond.

"I hope you like it." He grins.

I wrap both hands around the cup, the heat spreading through my palms like my fire used to do.

Before I know it, we've walked all the way to the park in the center of downtown. A memory of my first day in East Gate and the girls sitting on a blanket in the grass as my dad and I drive by flashes through my mind.

"It's different at night, right?" he asks with a charming grin, pulling me from my vivid memory.

I twist around, taking in the panoramic view of the bluff we had parked above, hardly seeing the road that led us there. The rolling hills, their brownish hue standing out more than earlier, reminding me of the changing cycles of the earth and my momentary connection to the elements.

The hills are bathed in a warm, golden light as the sun descends in the sky, just as Callen so lovingly referred to as the golden hour.

"It's something special," I respond.

Callen gently wraps his hand around my wrist. "Come on, this way." He leads me past the tall, green, weathered-looking clock.

Fallen leaves litter the ground, blazing with various vivid

shades of red and gold. They crackle under our feet as we stroll through the grass.

As we walk under the towering old maple trees, more leaves flutter down around us. So much for not leading Callen on. This feels like a date. It's like poetry coming to life.

The night is so idyllic; it's as if Callen orchestrated this moment—the peaceful night, the gentle breeze blowing through the trees, and the perfect timing of the golden hour. If he still had his magic, I'd be questioning him.

I finally take a sip of my drink. "This is delicious." The words roll smoothly off my newly warmed tongue. Bits of nutmeg and other spices cling to my tastebuds.

Add another win for Callen and his perfect night.

"Mrs. Maples knows what she's doing," I add.

"And she's good at reading people too. I think she knows what she's talking about. She called us a couple." He winks at me as he continues to lead us to the steps of the white gazebo in the middle of the park.

"You know, I always thought this would be a beautiful place to get married," he says, staring up at the old structure.

Married!

Is he seriously tossing around the marriage word right now?

Back that ass up, mister.

I ignore the comment, hoping he moves on to something else.

But he doesn't.

"This gazebo is as old as the town. I always thought that if this could withstand the test of time, so could anyone that vowed their love here."

Well, shit. That's romantic.

He reaches up and scratches the back of his neck. "I just mean—someday." He chuckles. "But then again, who knows where life will lead me."

An image of Callen in a crisp white groom's suit flickers through my mind, but I quickly let it evaporate. An icky feeling that I'm doing something wrong settles in my tummy.

Riley.

Will this feeling of guilt ever pass?

I mean—look at him. Callen is perfect and sweet and funny. AND hot as hell! He likes me, and I can't keep denying my feelings for him.

Callen's velvety eyes meet mine, but still, all I can think of is Riley's once-baby-blue eyes twinkling in the moonlight at Sam's party. Oh, and the unread text message burning a hole in my back pocket. I swear my phone is literally lighting my ass on fire. I pat my pocket to make sure it's not, but all is good.

Callen gives me a curious grin. I ignore the need to respond. He won't understand or want to understand because it has to do with Riley. Especially when he was so vulnerable with me, and I ignored him.

What's wrong with me?

My heart's torn into two pieces—one side with Riley's name and the other Callen's.

"Take a seat." He gestures toward the top step.

I set my drink down and tug at the sleeves of my sweater, stretching it to cover my cold hands.

Callen notices, because of course he does—he's always

watching me. I used to think it was creepy, but now I realize he's being sweet and attentive.

He takes off his jacket again and wraps it around me. This time, he lets his hands linger on my shoulders as he presses down the fabric against my back. He eases down beside me, then shifts his body to face mine.

"Izzy, I have something I want to ask you." His jaw is tense with apprehension.

Oh no, here it comes—the girlfriend talk.

I'm not ready.

Riley. Callen. Riley. Callen. Ugh!

He takes a deep breath, and his eyes flutter rapidly. "I was wondering if I could take you to your senior homecoming. I think we'd have a lot of fun together."

"Oh. Homecoming."

Not asking me to be his girlfriend.

I'm still not ready for this question either.

Think, Izzy, think!

"I don't have a dress. Plus, they cost too much."

He scrunches his nose. "I'm not sure if that's a yes or a no."

"It's an 'I don't have a dress, so I'm not going.' But thanks for the offer to take me." I shift uncomfortably on the steps.

"You can borrow one from Tahlia." His voice is plagued with desperation.

"I don't think Tahlia would want me wearing one of her dresses; plus, she's like a size or two smaller than me."

"Fine. Then I'll buy you one."

"It's not just the dress. I don't think I want to go," I respond.

Lies.

Riley's unread text is torturing me. I can't let go of the hope that he's had a change of heart and is finally coming to his senses. He may be texting me to say he's exploring methods to control his impulses, like what Bree did with Barrett. If that's the case, then I owe Riley the dance, not Callen. I can't make any decisions until I check my phone.

His eyes fall to the ground.

"I'll think about it," I quickly respond.

"Beswick, when will you finally realize we're meant for each other?" The question escapes his lips in a barely audible whisper.

"Callen, don't." I put my hand on his. "It's not that easy."

"Riley?" he questions.

A lump rises in my throat as my heart clenches with uncertainty. It's time to pull the band-aid off and admit I'm holding out for Riley. My mouth parts, waiting for the words to come out, but nothing does.

"Riley," he repeats. His finger points straight ahead. "Riley—he's right there, watching us again."

My mouth falls open, and my breath comes out panicky.

Riley's eyes glint maliciously in the golden light; his gaze is unrelenting with anger written all over his face.

"I'm going to go over there and say something to him."

I put my hand across his chest. "I don't think you should. I didn't want to ruin our night, but he texted me earlier."

"What! Izzy, you should have told me. What did it say?"

"I didn't check it."

"Why the heck not?"

"I didn't want you to be mad and have it ruin our night."

I keep my eyes on Callen, who is staring at Riley, and pull my phone from my pocket.

"Beswick, this could be important. He's been acting odd. He might be threatening you. We need to stay vigilant, remember?"

"Threatening me?" I question.

The thought never crossed my mind. Confessing his undying love for me, yes. But threatening me, no.

The divide in my heart pulsates as the crack becomes more evident—*Callen or Riley*—each side tugging to win the battle.

This is it. My moment of truth. Does Riley still love me?

My breath catches in my throat.

With one hand, I unlock my phone and swipe to view the message. It's long, but five words stare me straight in the face, and just like that, the Riley half of my heart plummets into my rib cage, leaving the Callen side to bleed out.

Five words—I WANTED YOU TO DIE.

"He—he wanted me to die." The words roll off my tongue fast and hot.

"Run, Beswick. Run!" Callen shouts.

CHAPTER 08
FOREVER DAMAGED

Run. Callen's words register in my head, but my body remains unresponsive.

Riley wanted me to die.

Waves of terror and sorrow flood every ounce of my being.

"You're a fucking dead man, Riley Hawkins," Callen shouts, leaping to his feet. A blur of his body catches in my peripheral view.

"Izzy, fucking run!" he shouts back mid-stride.

Both men who hold a piece of my heart sprint toward one another at an astonishing speed until the sound of their bodies colliding rocks me from my trance.

"Callen! Riley!" I scream.

Despite my desire to stay and try to pry them off each other, I quickly rise to my feet and take off in the other direction, only slowing to glance over my shoulder to make sure they're not really killing each other. After all, it's witch against hunter. Even if my soul is screaming at me to turn back, I suppress the urge and obey Callen.

I move toward the massive green clock and take refuge

there, hiding from view. I bend my knees and lower myself to the ground.

Quietly, I peek around the large monument worn down by years of weathering. The green paint is so fragile that it peels wherever I touch it.

My divided heart aches as I witness Callen and Riley attacking each other.

Callen's actions to protect my honor stir up a mix of emotions inside me. I never thought Riley was capable of such intense hatred. I mean, he's a hunter, but shouldn't his feelings for me run deeper than that? Shouldn't a part of him still feel like himself?

Without looking, I pull out my phone to read the rest of the message. As my eyes fall to the screen, the sharp sound of fists connecting with flesh reverberates through the air, sending shivers down my spine. My heart races as I cringe at the harsh, grating sound, causing my phone to slip from my hand, my fingers clumsily swiping across the screen before the device crashes to the ground with a loud thud.

Shit!

I retrieve my phone, keeping my eyes pinned on the boys. Callen is half-crouched, his arms extending outward and circling Riley. His lips curl upward with anger raging through his face. He rushes Riley, tackling him to the ground. Riley howls as Callen's knuckles meet his cheek. In retaliation, Riley returns the punch and flips Callen over.

"Stay the hell away from us," Callen warns, reversing Riley onto his back.

Riley rolls away from Callen and jumps to his feet, his

brown hair swaying. "I saw you two."

"So what?" Callen responds boldly.

"There's something going on, isn't there?" Riley accuses, his words dripping with fury.

He does care?

"What if there is? You hate her." With a determined look on his face, Callen pulls his right arm back, clenching his fingers into a fist. He takes a deep breath and braces himself for the second round of the fight.

"You're right. I don't care," Riley puffs.

And just like that, my heart slips back into the pit of my stomach.

"You can have her." Riley's muscular arms form a protective barrier, shielding himself from the vicious blow coming at him.

Callen leans in, and Riley instantly reacts by pivoting.

"I can do this all night, bro," Callen says.

"You witches belong together," Riley huffs. "You're not worth my time right now, witch." Riley's eyes burn with the fury of a hunter, visible even from afar, the darkness tightening its grip around him.

Callen slowly lowers his arms; his gaze locks on Riley as he gives him an out. Riley doesn't hesitate and takes off sprinting toward Main Street, his feet pounding hard against the pavement. Callen stands still, watching him go without looking back; his expression is unreadable.

I finally glance down at my phone; only the corner of the screen is cracked, but it somehow powered down during the fall.

Thank goodness.

I press the power button. My heart races as I anxiously wait for the screen to come to life, eager to read the rest of the message from Riley. I know I need to be quick, as Callen could catch me at any moment. The anticipation of what the rest of the message might say fills me with fear. I take a deep breath and try to steady my nerves as I finally see my home screen appear.

No, this can't be happening.

Where did it go?

I click buttons on my screen, hoping for a different outcome.

Fuck!

When it fell from my grip, I must have accidentally swiped something and deleted it. This time, there was no magic involved. It was entirely my fault—a big, fat Izzy mistake.

Ugh!

Maybe it's for the best.

He wanted me to die.

No good can come from seeing how much my ex-boyfriend hates me now.

Hunter or not, he's still Riley Hawkins, and his heart has turned to stone for me.

We're forever damaged, and it breaks my heart.

Overwhelmed with emotions, I slowly turn around and let the tears that have pooled in my eyes flow profusely like an open floodgate. The salty droplets stream down my face, leaving a trail of dampness as they fall. My body trembles with every sob, and I struggle to catch my breath as the tears continue to pour out of me.

Footsteps skate through the leaves, and Callen drops

down next to me. He pulls me into his arms, enveloping me in a full sense of comfort. His tenderness opens me up even more, and I cry uncontrollably into his shoulder until I have no more tears left inside of me.

Callen stands and extends his hand to help me up. My dainty hand falls into his, and he tenderly tugs me upward.

"I can't take you home like this. Your dad will worry if he sees you crying. Let's walk it off."

I nod, my vision blurred through the tears.

We walk back to the gazebo, stopping to collect his jacket that must have fallen off me while running.

"Why was he following us?" I ask, my voice trembling with panic.

Callen glances downward. "My guess is that Riley was here to hurt you." His words come out soft.

I tense at the mention of his name, which used to give me butterflies in my stomach.

"Oh," is all I can say.

Riley freed my heart tonight. I'm no longer his.

My eyes brim with tears again, making Callen appear blurry. He reaches up and gently wipes them away.

"Izzy, even without my magic, I'll keep you safe."

With those words, I know where my heart belongs.

"I know, Callen." I sniffle. Callen guides us up the steps, and we both bend down to pick up our abandoned drinks. I take a sip from mine; it's cold now, but it still tastes good. He leads me into the middle of the gazebo and plops down. I join him. Both of us lie on our backs, letting the cool air circle around us, drying up my tears.

I allow myself a few calming breaths when something catches my eye.

"What's that?" I ask, pointing at a curious drawing beneath the railing.

"I'm not sure. Probably some stupid kids graffitiing up the place. Jerks."

"No, I think it's a pentagram."

We scoot closer to the drawing.

I gulp. "It is a pentagram."

CHAPTER 09
TAINTED

A perfect circle with a star in the middle, a witch's pentagram, is drawn on the dirty white paint of the gazebo with an X marked through it.

My eyes are fixed on the drawing; the small words surrounding it render me speechless.

THE CHOSEN ONE MUST DIE

The word die is in red paint, with the letter e dripping like blood, creating a chilling effect.

My body stiffens.

Riley's words, 'I wanted you to die,' are as fresh as this paint.

"Izzy, this is a threat against you. You're the chosen one. Isobel said, 'The chosen one must come' in her diary, and the rival coven said they needed 'the chosen one' too. That's you."

We stand watchful, our heads swiveling as we peer out in all directions within the beautiful circular structure now tainted with hate.

I doubt he'll want to get married here now.

"Who did this?" My voice trembles, feeling I already know

the answer, but hoping Callen will have a different one.

Callen's hand instinctively goes to his already bruising cheek as he says, "My bet's on Riley."

I frown, agreeing.

"Does it hurt?" I ask, my hand hovering near his cheek.

He winces and pulls away from my touch, his eyes expanding in dread. "It's not me I'm worried about; it's you. We need to go. Now!"

"Sitting ducks," I respond, nodding.

"Exactly! Let's hurry back to the car." Callen quickly takes a photo of the evidence with his phone.

We descend the steps and cross through the park, the once-pretty leaves now becoming a nuisance to kick our way through as we quicken our speed.

"I'm sorry tonight turned out so awful," he huffs.

"It wasn't all awful," I grab his hand, interlacing his fingers in mine.

He twists his head and grins. Then we take off in a full sprint, our hands remaining locked firmly together, sending tingles through my body until we reach the car parked in front of a fully packed Mrs. Maples.

Once inside the car, Callen locks the doors. He shoots a protective glare at me. "What if it's not Riley? I'm not saying he's innocent, but what if—"

"It's the girl from this morning—Scarlet?" I choke out the words, finishing his sentence.

He nods. "Maybe you're right about her. We haven't heard hunters use those words. Now that I'm thinking about it, Riley wasn't in the room with the diary, and he wasn't in the forest when the rival coven uttered those exact words, calling for the chosen one. I mean, maybe he's still guilty; we can't count him out. But we don't know what Elizabeth Crowley or the Dark Mother—whatever we're calling her— had planned for her hunters. I'll ask my mom if she ever heard the word, but I doubt it, since she doesn't necessarily follow the hunter's path."

"But Tim does."

"We can't ask Tim. He'd cover for his son."

"Oh, right." I frown. "I guess this is turning out to be another Izzy problem."

"Izzy and Callen." He yanks his seatbelt on and starts the car. "We need to pull a freak show teatime repeat," he says, pulling onto the street. "I'm sneaking into your house after your dad goes to bed. If you were still talking to the girls, I'd have you sleep at my house. I'm sure they would understand in these circumstances, but it's getting late, and we need to have a plan. This will work for tonight—it has to."

When Callen pulls up to my house, the living room lights are on. The soft glow from inside makes my house look even creepier at night.

"My dad's still up, and he'll want to chat, especially since I missed dinner. I feel so bad. He's been alone since Anna is gone, and Tim is avoiding him at my stern request. He needs a new friend. I think it's time to call Jonathan Kent."

"Don't you think you have enough on your plate?"

"You're probably right, but if we've learned anything lately, it's that life's too short to sit around and wait."

"You're right about that," he agrees.

"I'll text you when it's OK to sneak in."
"Sounds good, Beswick. See you on the inside."

CHAPTER 10
BURNING REFLECTIONS

"Dad, I'm home."

"In the living room, sweetie," Dad's carefree voice echoes into the foyer.

I drop my bag at the door, then check myself in the hall tree mirror.

As I'm tucking my hair behind my ears, the familiar jingle of the older TV show, *Everybody Loves Raymond*, carries into the foyer. My dad's hearty chuckle rings out a moment after the laugh-track, following the first joke right on cue.

His giddiness for an episode he's probably seen ten times or more makes me smile. But my flat smile remains fixed in the mirror, not the full grin I feel spreading across my face. I shake my hands at my side, but the image continues to go unchanged, almost frozen in time.

My heart pounds wildly.

This is a good sign.

Could Gran-gran or Anna be trying to connect with me again? Do they know about Riley's text or the threatening drawing? Is this them reaching out to me finally?

Taking a deep breath, I wait to be transported back to the in-between world, or other realm as Callen called it, just like my first day in this creepy old house.

Nothing.

I sigh in defeat.

Who am I kidding? I don't have my magic and nothing like this has happened since that day in the forest. Well, except for the girl's touch this morning.

I hastily roll up my sleeve to check out my healing burn from Scarlet. The scar is gone. There is no evidence of it whatsoever. I run my hand over my skin to make sure, but it's completely healed, like it never happened.

Bringing my attention back to the mirror, I remove my hand from my arm. In my reflection, orange and red flames rise from my skin. The blaze dances high into the air, creating shadows on everything around me. The scent of charred skin makes me want to gag.

"Izzy, I thought you were coming in," Dad hollers.

Staring at my fiery reflection, I respond, "Yes. Be right there." My words are slow and controlled.

I frantically peel my gaze away from the mirror, and everything is as it was—normal and not on fire. I pat my arm to extinguish the non-existent flames and yank my sweater sleeve down.

Thirty-seven days of nothing, and now all of this at once.

I shake my arms at my sides, trying to release the weight of the day's events from my body. It's check-in time with my dad, the man who has no idea he's somehow folded up in this mess I'm trying to hide.

In the next room, Dad's comfortably settled on the old plush and cushy couch, or as Gran-gran used to call it, the davenport. Although, I never understood why. I'm sure if I ask my dad, he'd tell me, but that's a question for another day. Perhaps a day when someone isn't trying to kill me.

He has a TV tray pulled up in front of him with a steaming hot plate of leftover roast beef and noodles. I settle in the door frame, my body resting casually.

"Hey, Dad." I tug at my sweater sleeves.

Dad glances up at me and smiles. "Hey, kiddo."

"Sorry I missed dinner with you tonight. Callen wanted to take me to a few of his favorite places. Have you heard of Mrs. Maples?"

Good job, Izzy. Keep up the everything is fine and dandy ruse. But for the love of God, quit fidgeting.

"Oh yeah, that place. A guy I work with was telling me about it. Sounds like we've been missing out by only visiting here in the summer."

"I think you're right," I respond, trying to keep myself from falling apart.

Dad shovels a heaping spoonful of noodles into his mouth. "Please tell me you ate something for dinner?" he says in between bites.

"Um. No. We were too busy."

Too busy being followed and having my heart crushed.

"Well, if I would have known that, I wouldn't have taken all the leftovers. Go grab a plate. I can share what's left."

"It's OK, Dad. I can make a sandwich. Is there still some lunch meat in the fridge?"

"I think so. But you'll need to check the bread. It might be expired."

My tummy grumbles.

"OK. Will do. Are you staying up long?"

"Nah, heading to bed soon. I have an early morning planned tomorrow. The home repairs are never ending."

I smile. "I think I'm going to go make that sandwich now and eat it in my room."

"All right, sweetheart."

In the kitchen, I do a quick mold check as the bread is a few days past its expiration; all is good. I throw together two turkey and cheese sandwiches, one for me and one for my overnight guest.

I scour the cabinet, searching for something easy to pair with my pitiful entrée. A bag of microwave popcorn is the only thing that jumps out at me. I toss the bag in the old microwave that looks like it's the first one ever invented and wait for the kernels to pop.

Dad rounds the corner and sets his plate in the sink.

"Do you want me to do the dishes?" I ask.

"Nah, leave them. I'll get to them in the morning."

"Is your show over?" I eagerly ask.

"Yup. Heading up to bed now."

"OK. See you in the morning."

The ding on the microwave sounds, and I reach in to grab the steaming bag, pinching the top corner. When I turn around, Dad's gone.

Perfect.

I text Callen.

Izzy: All clear. Meet you in the hallway.
Callen: See you soon.

I pour the freshly popped popcorn into a large blue bowl and carefully balance my plate of sandwiches on top of it. I gracefully reach into the refrigerator and pull out two sparkling waters.

Callen is slowly closing the door, wincing at each creak when I creep up behind him.

"Boo," I say softly into his ear.

He twists around. "Shit, Beswick. I thought I was busted."

"My dad's in his bedroom. That whole separate wing of the house thing comes in handy when sneaking boys in."

"Oh, you do this often," he taunts.

"Only with you," I grin, shoving the drinks into his hand. "I made us a snack."

"Thank goodness. I'm dying for some food." He rubs his stomach.

"It's not much, so don't get too excited. It's all I could find."

"I'm not picky," he says, reaching under my carefully balanced plates, producing a handful of popcorn that he proceeds to stuff into his mouth. "Well, it's better than nothing, I suppose." He smiles and heads up the staircase.

With one foot hitting the second-floor landing, he takes a pause, but I nod, urging him to continue up the windy staircase.

He eyes me quizzically.

"I want to show you something first," I respond.

"My interest is piqued, Beswick." He quickly rotates on his heels and follows me.

Standing outside the third-floor door with my back protectively against it, I take a deep breath. "Something happened to me when I got home. Remember how I told you about my experience with the Victorian hall tree mirror on my first day here?"

"Yes, of course, that old antique in your foyer?"

I nod. "Well, I saw something again."

"Without your magic?" His voice is hopeful.

"Yes. In my reflection, I saw my arm burning where Scarlet touched me today."

"Are you serious?"

My heart thumps rapidly in my chest, and I nod.

"I want to show you my Gran-gran's secret room. The place where everything started for me and the girls."

"I can't believe you haven't brought me up here before. Why now?"

"I want to try something with you," I tell him.

A flicker of excitement passes over his face as his brow rises with curiosity.

With a twist of the knob, I open the door to my sacred place and invite Callen inside.

The last time I was up here was the day after the forest, and I haven't been back since. The thought is unsettling and makes me shudder.

I place our dinner next to the door, and without an explanation, I walk over to my hide-a-hole. Callen's eyes follow my movement, but he doesn't speak. I pull up the loose floorboards and retrieve my spellbook, Isobel's diary, and a bag of my witchy belongings.

I gesture for Callen to follow me to the attic door in the corner of the room. I attempt to balance the spellbook in my hand as I reach into the hollowed hole for the key.

When Callen approaches from behind, he's so close that his warm breath tickles my neck. The old wooden steps protest loudly as he waits for me to twist the key. The hinges groan when I push the door open, revealing my dimly moonlit space.

The room is an embarrassing mess, with scattered candles, spilled salt, and a blood-crusted offering bowl— evidence of my unsuccessful attempt to call upon my magic. I don't remember leaving the room in such disarray, but then again, I wasn't in the best headspace.

I struggle to hold back my tears, but I do my best to keep them from falling.

"So, this is where it all started?" Callen enters the room, his eyes searching the dimly lit space. He takes a moment, squinting and adjusting to the darkness as he surveys his surroundings.

The sound of his footsteps echoes against the walls, adding to the already eerie atmosphere of the room. Despite the darkness, he moves with purpose, his body language conveying a sense of determination and focus. "This place needs a cleanse," he says.

I hand him my bag of supplies. He eagerly sifts through it, his fingers grazing each item until he finds what he's looking for—the sage.

"I sense something ominous, even without my magic. What did you do here last time?"

I lower my head, feeling a deep sense of embarrassment. My cheeks flush with shame, and my eyes glance downward, unable to meet his gaze.

"The day after the forest, I decided to perform a spell, hoping to find a way back to our magic, so we could help Tahlia and Riley. As part of the spell, I made an offering, hoping my intentions would be heard and answered."

"You did what?" he interrupts.

"I know. It was stupid. It obviously didn't work."

"Izzy, I can't believe you did a spell like that alone. Remember what happened to Jessa because she wasn't a witch? What if something like that happened to you because you don't have your magic?"

"I'm still a witch, just a witch without powers. I wasn't afraid."

"Well, maybe you should have been. You have no idea what could have happened," he responds.

I puff out a hot breath. "I had to try. I couldn't accept that the rival coven stole our magic. Do you mean to tell me you haven't tried anything?"

"I didn't see the point. I knew it was gone." He shakes his head. "I can never stop worrying about you, can I?"

I'm not some fragile little creature.

He picks up my offering bowl. "Seriously, Izzy. You could have really hurt yourself."

A chance I was willing to take.

I release a deep sigh, feeling the weight of his unwillingness to understand.

"So, what did you want to try?" he asks.

"Well, now I'm not so sure I want to tell you." I cross my

arms under my chest and produce an exaggerated pout.

I take a deep breath, buying myself a moment before letting my silly little idea fly out of my mouth. "I had an ounce of hope given to me downstairs when I gazed into the mirror. I wanted to see if together, maybe we could"—I force my gaze downward—"try again."

He pivots around and rushes out of the attic, his footsteps echoing in the deafening silence.

So, is that a no?

I'm shocked when he reenters the room, with his mouth stuffed full of sandwich. He hands me mine. As he chews, he urges me to eat. "You'll need your strength if we're going to attempt this."

So, not a no.

I eagerly accept the sandwich and take my time eating it, while he finishes his in two more bites. He doesn't wait for me to begin. Instead, he lowers himself to the ground and cleans the circle, ensuring every inch inside of it is free from my previous mess.

He carefully lights each black candle, one by one, and arranges them in a perfect circle along Gran-gran's original chalk outline. The flames flicker high, casting a glow in the room. He then lights the sage with the last candle and moves throughout the attic counterclockwise. The pungent aroma trails behind him as he cleanses our space of negative energy.

I shove the last bite of my sandwich into my mouth, and he passes me the burning bundle. I cleanse my body from head to toe with it, circling it around me, ridding myself of a month's worth of hostile energy.

He repositions the offering bowl and places the spell book in the middle. Picking up the kitchen knife, he gives me a disapproving look, but refrains from lecturing me—he knows it's useless—and places it next to the bowl.

I pass the sage back to him, and he cleanses himself with it before extinguishing the burning bundle.

I stand still as he carefully picks up the spilled container of salt. He takes a pinch of it between his fingers, then proceeds to draw a straight line across the threshold of the doorway, ensuring the line is continuous and unbroken.

"What's that for?" I ask. "We already have our circle."

"Added protection. No one else may enter our space without invitation. But it's hard to say if it will work, since we're without our magic. Yes, the chalk technically does the same thing for our sacred circle, but you can never be too cautious. In my opinion, salt is always the safest. Plus, it doesn't hurt to add a second layer of protection."

"Aren't you just a bowl full of knowledge?"

A cunning grin plasters his face, making me think he enjoys being the expert in the room. Yet, I can't help but feel empathy for him. He's never been able to discuss magic with his father, the one person who was like him—that is, until recently. But even now, he has to be cautious with his questions.

As Callen finishes setting up our circle, I can't help but picture him doing his research and practicing magic alone in his bedroom. The thought breaks my heart, but I've been doing the same thing. We may be more alike than I realize.

"All right, Beswick. I think we're all set. We just might be the two dumbest witches that ever lived."

"Or the two smartest witches," I add.

"Well, here goes nothing."

CHAPTER 11
HERE GOES EVERYTHING

We both stand still, gazing at each other. His dark eyes lock on mine in confusion.

"Now what?" he asks.

"Oh, I thought you had a plan. You seemed to know what you were doing."

"I was simply setting the stage for you. I thought you had a plan."

"No, but I guess we can try the spell I crafted and see if it works now." I remove a folded-up piece of paper that I carefully tucked in between two pages of my spellbook.

I extend my arm toward him, holding the sheet of paper between my fingers. He grazes my hand during the hand-off, and my heart flutters with excitement for two very different reasons.

As he reads my spell, my heart sinks when he reaches the part about Riley and freeing my love from his anomaly. I'm slightly embarrassed, but what other choice did I have at that moment? I had to try.

He reaches into my bag, pulls out an ink pen, and starts

making corrections on the paper. He slips the newly crafted spell into the center of our circle and picks up the knife.

"You know what you have to do, right?"

I nod. "Picture the elements. Imagine everyone with their powers back."

He cuts into his hand and lets a drop of blood hit the bowl.

"Careful, only a small cut, Izzy."

I scratch the surface of my skin until a tiny drop of blood rushes to the surface. I ease my hand over the bowl and wait for it to fall.

"OK. Let's hope something happens. We would be a lot stronger with four."

"But we can't get them involved until we know for sure this is something we can do. We can't get anyone else's hopes up. Especially Tahlia's. Her birthday is getting closer every passing moment."

"Agreed. So, this has to work. I need my friends back."

"And we need help with whoever left that drawing for us to find."

"And Sam Hornsby, maybe," I add.

"And keeping Jessa quiet."

"And Scarlet."

"And. And. And. Shit, we've got a lot of problems," Callen responds, cupping both of my hands in his.

"Here goes everything."

"Earth. Air. Fire. Water. Earth. Air. Fire. Water. Earth. Air. Fire. Water." With each repetition, we hope to feel a surge of energy flowing through us, just as before.

We pause, feeling nothing between us besides our

undeniable chemistry—a magnetic pull that I can't lie to myself about anymore. It's not just a passing moment of magic, but something deeper within our souls.

"It's time to begin—to call forth the magic that has been taken away from us. Let's get it back."

"Hail to the guardians of mother earth, air, fire, and water.
We summon you to hear our plea.
We ask for your help to invoke thee.
Our magic is gone.
Bring it back to where it belongs.
Let fire and water find us whole.
Accept our offering bowl.
Bless our sisters with their gifts.
Bring our coven back to full rich.
We trust you to hear our plea.
Please help us, for we invoke thee.
We invoke thee.

So shall it be."

We stand frozen, our eyes locked in a wordless exchange. The air is charged with anticipation as we both hold our breath, afraid to disrupt our spell's fragile, unknown state. Each passing second feels like an eternity as we wait for something—anything—to happen.

I have no magic, no fire—nothing. It's just like last time.

Callen's come to the same realization as me. It's written across his face—we failed.

A knock on the door startles us, causing me to drop Callen's hands.

"Oh, crap. Oh, crap. We're so busted." My heart pounds in my chest as panic ripples through my insides. "How am I going to explain this?"

"Be right there, Dad," I call out.

I cautiously step out of our circle, my breathing growing more rapid as I cross the small room.

My hand shakes with nerves as it rests on the door handle, but I don't get a chance to twist the knob. Callen's strong grip is pulling me away from the door. I twist around and gaze at him with confusion.

"Your dad doesn't even know you can get into this room. Why would he come searching up here for you?" he whispers.

I lift my shoulders and then release them while I consider his question.

"Something feels off in the air," he adds, keeping me pulled back.

"Dad?" I question.

No response.

"Dad?" I raise my voice.

Still nothing, but Callen's right; the air seems charged with an unexplainable energy.

"Stay here." He moves to the door, lending an ear to the old wood.

Slowly, he turns his head back to me, his eyes wide with fear. "Izzy, do you remember that spell in the forest? The ones the rival coven used to curse us and take away our magic?"

I nervously bite at the corner of my bottom lip until the

metallic taste of blood startles me. "Of course I do. It's been on repeat in my brain since that day."

He takes a deep gulp; his Adam's apple moves up and down his throat. "Same. Someone's chanting it behind this door right now." He presses his hand firmly against the weathered wood.

"Impossible," I respond, meeting Callen at the door. With bated breath, I press my ear against the surface.

On the other side of the door, their spell echoes through the room, its dark energy pulsing with each repetition.

"Tenebras invocamus. Expellant magicae ad infernos. Tenebras invocamus. Expellant magicae ad infernos. Tenebras invocamus. Expellant magicae ad infernos. Tenebras invocamus. Expellant magicae ad infernos. Tenebras invocamus. Expellant magicae ad infernos. Tenebras invocamus. Expellant magicae ad infernos."

"Is somebody there?" I ask, my voice trembling with fear.

The air between us is thick with darkness, and the uncertainty of our situation is assembling like bricks, keeping us prisoners in the attic.

No one answers my question, and the spell keeps going. It's never-ending. It's as if it has a life of its own.

"Tenebras invocamus. Expellant magicae ad infernos. Tenebras invocamus. Expellant magicae ad infernos. Tenebras invocamus. Expellant magicae ad infernos. Tenebras invocamus. Expellant magicae ad infernos. Tenebras invocamus. Expellant magicae ad infernos. Tenebras invocamus. Expellant magicae ad infernos."

"What do we do?" My voice trembles.

"Did we cause this to happen?" he asks, wiping away the beads of sweat on his forehead.

"I-I don't know," I stutter, the words getting caught in my throat. "I've heard this spell for thirty-seven days, but only in my head. Never out loud like this."

"Same."

"Callen, you never told me you were hearing their chant."

"I didn't want to worry you. I thought it was only me."

"Well, if we're both hearing it, Tahlia, Margo, and your dad must be hearing it too," I respond.

"We need to get out of here."

"Can whatever is on the other side of that door hurt us, do you think? It can't really be them; they're dead," I say.

"I think the only way to find out is to open the door and see for ourselves."

"Stay here," a voice commands, the words echoing off the walls and sending shivers down my spine.

I slowly turn around, my eyes scanning the dimly lit space.

But there's no one in sight. I fold into Callen's protective arms, together breathing as one.

"Isobel? Anna?" Callen calls out.

"It's not them. That's not their voice."

CHAPTER 12
STAY

I try to steady my breath and calm my nerves, but it's useless. Our magic's still gone. The spell failed, and now we're under attack.

"There's no way we're staying here," Callen says urgently, his words echoing my own thoughts.

As he steps back from me, I shift to meet his gaze. The terror in his wide eyes unnerves me. His hand is already on the door handle, ready to flee.

I don't argue with him. I agree; we need to get out of this attic as soon as possible. Something doesn't feel right.

My heart's pounding, waiting for him to free us from this room, but also fearing what's waiting for us on the other side.

"I said stay," the voice commands us. Its ghostly tone penetrates deep into my bones, causing goosebumps to line my arms.

"The door handle won't budge." A note of panic creeps through Callen's voice as he twists the handle again and pushes on the door.

"You've got to be kidding me. Let me try." I twist, but the

handle remains stubbornly still, refusing to yield to either of us.

"Wait it out," the voice requests.

Fear kinks through my stomach, knotting and twisting until I feel ill inside. "Who are you, and what do you want with us?"

No response.

Callen and I collapse along the length of the door, our bodies heavy with defeat.

The chant continues, ceasing to ease up. *"Tenebras invocamus. Expellant magicae ad infernos."*

"Looks like we're waiting this out," he says.

The door begins to violently rattle, shaking both of us.

"Let us in. Let us in." The words are airy and lifeless, yet menacing and desperate at the same time.

"We know you're in there." A mixture of Mrs. Jamison, Dale, Darla, and Robin's voices blend together in a devilish tone.

"We really messed up, didn't we?" I ask.

"I don't know how we could have done this if we didn't get our magic back. Our spell shouldn't have worked. I don't think this is our fault."

"What do you want from us?" I cry out.

"The chosen one," the devilish tone responds.

My body trembles. *They want me.*

Callen proceeds to silence me, laying his finger against my lips. "Don't respond. Maybe if we stay quiet, they'll disappear and go back to whatever realm they came from."

Even with the impending fear of being hunted by the

ghosts of the rival coven, my insides quiver from his touch. I can't resist the pull toward him and lean into his embrace, feeling safe and protected. I rest my head on his strong shoulder as we sit silently, waiting. The only sound that breaks through their chanting is our synchronized breathing as we hold each other tightly.

"I'm glad you're here with me, Callen."

"I wouldn't be anywhere else, Beswick."

CHAPTER 13
MEET-CUTE

I wearily rub my tired eyes and take a deep breath, trying to shake the intense grogginess flooding my head.

Where am I?

I try to make sense of my scattered memories, pulling them into focus, but a heavy fog of confusion remains.

Rubbing my eyes once more, I notice the black candles that have dwindled to the last bit of wax.

Oh my gosh—the attic—we fell asleep.

I shift my gaze downward, and I'm met with the sight of Callen's toned arm wrapped gently around my waist.

I softly nudge him. "Get up," I whisper.

Callen pulls me close to him with a firm grip, pressing our bodies closer together, his head nestling into my hair.

He slowly raises his arms above his head, his strong muscles stretching and flexing as he takes a deep breath and lets out a satisfyingly long yawn.

I twist to observe his facial expression change as he recalls where we are.

"Oh, crap! Are they still out there?" He leaps up, leaving

me on the cold, dusty floor.

He presses his ear against the door and gently turns the handle.

It opened.

He pokes his head through the narrow opening and scans the room before softly calling out, "Hello?" He pauses, waiting for a response that never comes, and turns back to me. "I think it's safe for us to leave. Whatever was behind this door is gone—for now."

"Good. We need to sneak you out before my dad gets up. He'll freak if he catches you here. We can figure this whole nightmare out once I get you out of this house."

We tiptoe down the stairs, trying not to make any noise. I guide Callen to the front door, practically shoving him outside, but he pokes his head back in.

"Take a shower. I'll be back in an hour to pick you up. We can't keep this information to ourselves any longer. I'll brief my family, but I think it's crucial that we're all together today. Perhaps even Jessa should be there too, but that's for Margo to decide."

"Is that Callen?" my dad says, sneaking up behind me, scaring me half to death.

Busted.

"You're here bright and early," he says.

If only Dad were more observant, he would surely notice the tangled mess of my hair and repeated outfit, and realize that I'm sneaking a boy out of the house and not letting him in.

Thank goodness for his obliviousness.

Callen reaches up and rubs the back of his neck.

"Morning, Mr. Beswick. I-I thought I'd swing by and see if I could take Izzy out for breakfast." He stumbles for his words. "The Bistro on 4th has amazing pancakes."

Good save, Callen.

"Call me Steven. I feel so old when you kids call me Mr. Beswick. I would say the age-old joke of 'that's my father's name,' but since I don't know my father, that one doesn't work for me." He chuckles.

Callen and I exchange a surprised glance.

My dad never brings up his father. Maybe losing his mother brought up some underlying things he was repressing. Good thing I'm working on it for him.

He gestures for Callen to come inside. "Don't go spending your hard-earned money on food."

Dad ushers us into the kitchen. I want to scream and tell him to leave us be, but I don't. Instead, I let my dad continue.

"I was about to make a big breakfast before starting my house repairs. I have to patch—"

I interrupt him. "Dad, I don't think Callen cares about our decrepit home and all of its problems."

"No, it's OK, Izzy. I don't mind, but I don't want to intrude on your morning. I can take Izzy out for breakfast another day. Why don't the two of you have breakfast together?" Callen says sweetly.

Really, I know he's dying to get out of this house and talk with his family and the rest of our coven and explain to them what's going on and plead for their help.

"No, please join us. I insist." Dad pulls out a chair for Callen to take a seat.

"Dad, I don't think we have any pancake mix. Callen's craving pancakes."

"Good thing I know how to make them from scratch." Dad's eyes twinkle with excitement.

Don't cave, Callen. Stick to the plan.

"Well, if you're making them from scratch, I can't say no." Callen shrugs his shoulders in defeat and plops down into the open seat.

I slide into the chair next to him, giving Callen my classic Izzy stare down. "There better be bacon, too," I add, succumbing to the power of my dad's persuasion.

A smirk plays across my dad's face. "I'm not some kind of monster, Izzy. Of course, there will be bacon. He grabs eggs, bacon, milk, and butter from the fridge and places them on the counter.

He walks to the pantry and pulls several ingredients from the middle shelf. "Hey, I saw posters displayed all around town of Jessa, and I assume, her parents. Is her dad really running for mayor? I keep forgetting to ask you."

"Yup," I respond.

"You should have told me."

"It's not like I've ever met the man," I huff.

I only saw him for the first time yesterday at a distance, and I'd like to keep it that way.

I flash Dad a blank stare. "It didn't cross my mind that you'd want to know."

"Well, tell Jessa, her dad has my vote."

I fake a half smile.

If I ever talk to her again.

"I think he's running unopposed, so he should win no matter what," Callen adds.

"Good, a nice clean race." Dad turns on the burner and adds several slices of bacon to the pan before returning to the counter to start the pancake mix. "I haven't seen the girls around lately."

There's a reason for that, but I can't tell you the truth or you'd hate me.

"Everyone's been very busy," I respond.

Just keep piling on the lies.

"Makes sense. Senior year has a way of pulling everyone in different directions. And speaking of that, Izzy please tell me you started your college applications. You're already so far behind."

"Yes, Dad. I applied to the schools we talked about."

More lies. I only applied to one because it was the easiest.

"What about you, Callen? Are you in college? Sorry I never asked until now."

"No, it's OK. I deferred a year. Trying to save up some extra income before I go into debt."

The real reason is that he was worried about his sister, but that's not a story for your ears.

"Smart boy. Just make sure you go next fall. A college education is so important."

"I agree," Callen responds. "I've already been accepted to the University of Connecticut, so if all goes to plan, that's where I'll be next fall."

"No way." I slug him in the arm. "You didn't tell me. That's my first choice."

My only choice.

Truthfully, I don't know a thing about the school I applied to, and I'm not excited whatsoever. Well, maybe I'm a little more excited now that Callen's going to be there.

"That will be nice. Izzy will have a friend if it all works out. Fingers crossed." Dad crisscrosses his two fingers and smiles. He then proceeds to take his time measuring out each ingredient before adding them to the bowl. As he stirs, a strange look spreads across his face. "I have to tell you about this strange dream I had last night. Maybe you two can help me decipher its hidden meaning." He laughs.

"A dream?" I question.

"I kept hearing the same thing in Latin or something. No, I'm sure it was Latin. I wish I could remember it. It was like someone was following me, chanting behind me in the forest out back, but every time I turned around, there was no one there. Isn't that an odd dream for a guy who usually doesn't dream?"

Callen strokes his chin that's grown a five o'clock shadow since last night. "That is strange." His brows tighten.

A tingling sensation flushes my body like tiny pinpricks. They're trying to get to my dad again. But what good is it to chant to a man who doesn't practice magic?

Ugh! Those darn witches and their dark magic taunting us from beyond their shallow graves. I want to scream in frustration, but I don't. Now would be as good of a time as any to tell him what he is, but my mouth won't open. Instead, I sit quietly in my chair, letting Callen deal with this one.

"Dreams are a funny thing. I never know what to make of them." Callen chuckles lightly, playing into the good actor I need him to be right now. "My dreams are never normal, so I don't try to give them a second thought once I wake up."

Dad shakes his head, contemplating Callen's useless answer. I mean, what was he supposed to say? 'Witches are summoning you and want to take the magic you don't know you have. Everything you think you know is a lie and has been your entire life.'

As my dad's attention shifts away from us, Callen's eyes widen and lock onto mine, his expression a mixture of WTF and we're screwed.

"Oh, crud. This isn't good," Dad shouts, frustration coating his voice, taking us out of our moment.

"What's not good, Dad?" I ask, but my eyes are immediately drawn to the puddle of water slowly approaching his blue slippers.

He pulls the hand towel that's hanging on the oven door and tosses it on the ground. It soaks up very little. He moves to the sink and opens the cabinet door below it.

"The darn pipe busted, and water is leaking everywhere. Izzy, can you go grab a bucket? There should be an empty one right out back. I'm going to go shut off the water. I'm pretty handy with most things, but I'm no plumber. Callen, can you watch the bacon?"

Callen gets up and mans the stove, while I walk out back. Sure enough, there's an empty white bucket leaning against the house just as Dad suggested. I bring it inside and place it under the leak.

Dad returns from wherever the water shut off is in this old house with his phone pressed against his ear. "I'm trying to call

Tim, but his phone keeps going to voicemail. I'm starting to feel like Tim is ghosting me. Did I use that right? Ghosting?"

Callen and I snicker.

Callen's brow rises, and a sly grin spreads across his face. I know exactly what he's thinking, and I shake my head in disagreement. He opens his mouth anyway.

"Steven, I know of a handyman in West Gate. I hear he's cheaper than all the ones here in East Gate. Let me pull up his information and see if he takes emergency calls." He smiles, showing his perfectly straight teeth.

My mouth falls open. I want to smack that grin right off his face. I can't help but feel a surge of betrayal.

Callen shakes his phone toward my dad. "It looks like this guy takes emergency calls. Should I submit a request for you?"

What is he doing? This isn't part of the plan.

Dad drops to the ground with a roll of paper towels and several hand towels. "Thanks, Callen. I appreciate the help. I suppose I should price shop, but I don't think I have time for that. Go ahead and submit the request. It's 1803 Jefferson Place—make sure you get the address correct."

"Got it," Callen says, plucking away at his screen.

Running water would be nice, especially since I have yet to shower, but not at the expense of my dad meeting his father for the first time in his life without me vetting him. What if he's a bad guy?

Dad tosses a sopping heap of paper towels into the trash can. "Izzy, my credit card is in my wallet if Callen needs it to confirm the request."

"OK, Dad," I respond, tugging Callen by his shirt sleeve into the dining room. "Dad, keep an eye on the bacon, we'll be right back," I holler.

"What are you thinking?" I slug him in the arm. "This isn't part of the plan. I wanted to check him out first—make sure he's not a creep or some hideous magical being that Anna fell for. You never freakin' know these days." I toss my hands in the air.

"I'm sure it's going to be OK. Your poor sweet dad has lost so much—let's give him his father. If he shows up and turns out to be a creep, you can hate me forever. You said it yourself that life is too short to sit around and wait. So, there's no time like the present. This is going to be the perfect meet-cute."

"Meet-cute?"

"You know, like in the movies, when two characters meet."

"Isn't that supposed to be a romantic thing? I think you got it wrong." I pop my hip and stick my tongue out.

"Either way, it's our chance to do something good for once. Put a little bit of good karma out into the world. Come on, Izzy, let them have their father-son meet-cute."

"Fine," I huff. "And only because I need running water again. You're not going anywhere. Our other problems will have to wait."

Callen grins. "You know we have a pretty epic meet-cute story. Boy meets girl at a coffee shop, then finds out he's her friend's older brother who has a massive secret. It's totally an epic friends to lovers story."

"In your dreams, Callen." I laugh.

"Always in my dreams, Beswick." He winks.

CHAPTER 14
A MIRACLE

An hour slowly passes as we wait for the man that my dying witch of a grandmother told me to contact while we were together in an in-between world for witches. My thoughts sound insane, but they're as real as the nails that I'm nervously biting.

Callen rubs my knee. "It's going to be OK."

"I hope so," I respond.

"Your dad makes some killer pancakes. I'm so stuffed," Callen says, sliding further back into the plush couch.

A loud knock erupts from the front door, the sound carrying into the living room, making us jump to our feet. My stomach falls.

"Oh, good. That was fast," Dad says, hurrying past us with a wet towel over his shoulder.

Callen and I eagerly follow behind with my nervous energy in tow.

Dad swings the door open, and there he is—my father's father, my grandpa.

"Hello, you must be"—the man looks down at his paper"—

Callen Latham-Hart." He pauses and stares up at the old house with a puzzled look on his face.

Dad waves him inside. "Come on in, sir. And that's my daughter's friend's name on your service request. My name is—"

The man cuts him off as he steps inside, a dazed look still plastering his oval-shaped face. "You know, I haven't been to this house in over forty years."

"Service call? Wow, you've been in the business a long time," my dad responds.

"No. I used to know the girl that lived here." He laughs uncomfortably. "We used to date."

My dad runs his fingers through his thick dark hair, mimicking the man's puzzled expression while deducing the facts.

Callen and I walk backward until we hit the bottom step and simultaneously drop down. If we had popcorn, it'd be like we were at the movies—the perfect meet-cute.

What was I so nervous about?

"Anna, her name was Anna Beswick. Such a looker she was." The handyman grins as if recalling her every feature.

Dad's jaw practically hits the floor. "That-that's my mother. You dated her?"

"Yes, I did," the man replies with a hard to read pressed smile.

Dad extends his hand to the man. "I'm Anna's son, Steven Beswick."

"Is that so," the man says, scratching at his short white beard.

"Please come in." Dad gestures. "How long did the two of you date, if you don't mind me asking?"

"Oh gosh, we dated for a while, then she just up and left town. She didn't even tell me she was leaving. That was the summer of '76—worst summer of my life." His eyes close, and his head falls heavy like he's been carrying around a weight with him for over forty years.

"Sorry to hear that." Dad frowns. "I knew she left town shortly after she found out she was pregnant with me. She said she wanted a better life for me than East Gate had to offer. I never understood why she thought that. I love it here. I suppose it's my fault she left."

"What's your birthdate? If you don't mind me asking," the handyman asks with a glimmer of hope dancing in his eyes.

Just wait for it.

"I was born January thirteenth, 1977."

"No, that can't be right." The man shakes his head.

Dad stares quizzically at him.

"No, that's not correct. It can't be. Anna left town in August of '76 after she miscarried our child. I always assumed that's why she left with zero notice—facing me— facing us, after a loss like that at such a young age. Of course, I didn't blame her, but things like that are never easy to face, let alone talk about." He scratches his head. "But that math doesn't add up, even if she conceived again right after her loss."

The two men stand motionless, their eyes searching each other's for answers. The moment it clicks, their eyes well with tears.

Took you long enough.

I almost wish I had tissues because I find myself welling with emotion too.

"This might sound crazy, and forgive me for asking, but do you know who your father is?"

Dad shakes his head slowly from side to side, dazed by the handyman's words.

The man gasps, bringing his heavily calloused hand to his mouth. "I think you might be my son. I think your mother owes me an explanation."

A single tear rushes down my dad's cheek. Dad tosses his hand in the air. "Oh my God. Wow, this is a miracle. I never thought I'd find you, and now here you are, standing right in front of me. But I'm so sorry to tell you this"—Dad chokes on his words—"my mother . . . she passed away last month. I don't think you're going to get that explanation."

He places his hand on my dad's shoulder and gives him a thoughtful squeeze. "Oh, man. I'm so very sorry for your loss. I didn't mean to sound disrespectful."

"Thanks. It was sudden. To be honest, I'm still trying to process it. The whole situation doesn't make sense."

This is the first I'm hearing of this. Dad never expressed his concern over Anna's death.

"What happened, if you don't mind me asking?"

"She fell in the woods out back and—" he trails off.

"That's awful."

"Yes, very."

"But I'd love to hear more about you. Oh, my goodness, I didn't even catch your name."

"It's Jonathan Kent."

"Jonathan, it's an absolute pleasure to meet you." Dad gestures for me to join them. "I'd like you to meet my daughter, Izzy."

"Wow, so you could be my grandpa," I say, smiling at him, knowing darn well he is.

"I guess we could do one of them DNA tests to find out for sure," Jonathan responds.

"I don't think you have to," Callen says, coming up from behind. "The three of you look like family. You're most definitely related."

"Jonathan, this is my daughter's friend, Callen. The one who put in the service request on my behalf."

"Nice to meet you, young man." Jonathan grabs Callen's hand and shakes it vigorously, as if it's his way of saying thank you for bringing him to his family.

My dad pulls me into a side hug. "Who would have thought a busted pipe could bring a family together? Always a silver lining." Dad gleams with excitement. He's practically glowing.

"Please come in. I want to hear all about your life. I have a pot of coffee that should still be warm. Please excuse the mess. We were in the middle of making breakfast when we noticed the leak."

I clear my throat. "Dad, this is super exciting news. I'm dying to find out more, but can we fix the pipe first, so we can turn the water back on? I'm also dying for a shower."

"You haven't showered yet, and you were going out for breakfast?" He gives me an accusatory stare.

"Where's the leak?" Jonathan asks, interrupting my near interrogation.

"Under the kitchen sink," Dad responds.

Jonathan pushes through us and navigates to the kitchen without any need for directions.

When we meet him in the kitchen, his head's already under the sink.

"Oh, this shouldn't be a hard one to fix. I have what I need in my van. But Steven, these old pipes won't last much longer. They're about to rust straight through, and I imagine it's not the only one in the house like this. I can do a quick fix, but this will need to be addressed soon."

Dad strokes his chin. "Let's do the quick fix, so my daughter can shower. Then we can make a plan to look at the rest of the plumbing. How does that sound?"

"Sure thing. Let me disassemble this first, then I'll go grab the piece I need from my work van." He tucks his head back under the cabinet. The sound of tools clinking against metal echo through the kitchen.

He pokes his head back out. "You know, when I was younger, people used to think this house was haunted, and by all the noises it's making now, I don't think I could disagree." He lets out a hearty laugh.

It's something like that, Jonathan Kent.

Callen and I exchange a nervous glance before we both let out a forced chuckle.

Callen checks his phone. "I suppose it's time for me to head home and let you three catch up and get acquainted. Izzy, I'll be back in a little while to pick you up, if that's

OK, Steven."

"Yes, that's fine, Callen."

"It was so great to meet you, Mr. Kent." Callen waves.

"I'd shake your hand, but—" he waggles his dirty fingers and nods toward Callen.

"I get it." Callen smiles, grabs his jacket, then disappears around the corner.

I slide into my chair at the kitchen table, my half-eaten plate of pancakes sitting in front of me. I listen as my dad asks Jonathan an endless loop of questions, which feels more like an interrogation. But it's nice to see my dad so excited. The two of them fit together perfectly. My dad doesn't need Tim Hawkins; he has his father now, a real handyman.

I listen as Jonathan tells my dad he's a widower with no children. His wife passed away fifteen years ago, and he never remarried.

My phone vibrates against the table, interrupting our impromptu family reunion.

Callen: We've got a problem.
Izzy: Ugh. When do we not have a problem?

Three green dots flicker on the screen.

Callen: You need to see this.

An image materializes on my screen, and a wave of terror floods my body. My hand falls limp, my phone crashing to the ground.

CHAPTER 15
BUSTED

Panic envelops me like a wildfire, starting in my toes and quickly spreading to my head, leaving me dizzy and unable to breathe.

Quickly, I bend down to retrieve my phone, avoiding the questioning gaze of my dad.

Glancing at the image again, I gasp and quickly cover my mouth. It's the same drawing as last night: a pentagram with the words THE CHOSEN ONE MUST DIE in red paint. The words blast me in the face, fueling my panic. This time, it's on Jonathan Kent's work van.

Great.

Something catches my eye, something that's different. I pinch the screen to zoom in. The word LIAR is in the bottom of the circle. I can almost feel the hate dripping from the paint.

Riley?

I shake the thought from my head.

"Please excuse me for a moment," My voice uncontrollably trembles.

"Is everything OK?" Dad asks.

"Yes, it's fine."

Jonathan Kent's curious gaze settles over me. I try to swallow, but my throat tightens.

Are you one of them, Mr. Kent?

"Be right back," I slowly back out of the kitchen, my heart thumping in my chest.

Once out of their sight, I dash out of the house and toward Jonathan's white work van, where Callen is waiting for me.

His eyes are fixed on the image painted just above the rear wheel well, facing the street side. Just like in the photo, the image oozes with threat, making me nauseous. Without words, I gesture to the new message.

Callen mouths the word 'liar' as if trying to process it for the first time. "I wonder what it means?"

"It means I'm not safe anywhere. Not even my own home. There's something more going on here than just dead witches haunting us and reminding us we're cursed."

"You're right." His shoulders sink, seemingly weighted by our constant defeat.

"I bet it's that girl. She was probably sent here to do the rival coven's dirty work," I respond, ready to point a finger at someone I know nothing about.

Callen rubs the back of his neck. "Or Riley. We can't completely count him out. He's out of control right now, and after that text he sent you . . ."

The thought alone is enough to make me physically ill, but hearing it out loud is more than I can handle.

"But you said it yourself last night—these words aren't hunter's words."

"I don't know everything, Izzy. My guess is as good as yours."

Callen swipes his finger, leaving a trail through the slick, thick red paint. "It's still wet." He flashes me his red stained finger. "See how fresh it is?"

My eyes swiftly scan the street, trying to catch our mysterious culprit, searching for any signs of movement, but there's hardly a soul in sight, only a little kid playing fetch with his dog down the hill. I'd hardly call him a suspect.

"They're gone. I already ran up and down the block." He takes his shirt sleeve and vigorously smears the rest of the drawing, making a mess of the van's side and his presumably expensive shirt. "We can't have people seeing this. We can't afford to let this message spread throughout the town. It could trigger a witch hunt. I should have thought to destroy the one in the gazebo last night. I'll do it on my way home."

"With what? It's already dry."

Callen carefully opens the back door of Jonathan's van. "Not locked." He smiles, then scans the back of the van, tucking a few items into his jacket. "People are way too trusting in small towns."

"There goes your karma points."

"It's keeping you safe, so I'll do what I have to do," Callen responds with his all too familiar hero's grin.

"Do you think Jonathan Kent did this?"

Callen laughs. "Izzy, are you serious?"

I purse my lips. "Yes. Dead serious. We don't know anything about him. This is why I wanted to vet him first, but you were all like, 'Let's make this perfect little meet-cute, blah, blah, blah,'" I say mockingly.

"Your dad's happy. Jonathan Kent isn't out to get us. Plus, this is fresh, and he wouldn't have vandalized his own property on the off chance you'd see it. Izzy, that doesn't make sense. Also, he didn't know you existed until an hour ago."

"Or did he?" I fire back.

My brain is walking through all the questions I don't have answers to, and it's making me exhausted.

I need more coffee.

"I think you're looking to blame anyone but lover boy. It's not your sweet new grandpa. Trust me."

My lips curl into a sneer, but Callen doesn't notice. Instead, both of our attention is drawn to the front door groaning as it swings wide open, the sound carrying down to us on the street, sending me into a full-blown panic.

"He's coming. Go," I plead, shooing Callen away.

"I'll be back soon, Beswick. Stay safe," Callen says before sprinting to his SUV discreetly parked down the street.

I scamper up the hill, narrowly avoiding Jonathan, who's slowly making his way down the many steps. I hide near the side of the house, peering out from behind the bushes, keeping a watchful eye on his movements, hoping he doesn't spot the vandalism and accuse us. That's the last thing I need.

Thankfully, Jonathan takes the sidewalk to the back of his van. He appears to be uneasy as he glances from side to side before pulling the door open, then disappearing inside. I'm about to run to the front door, but he reappears. As he's stepping out with a piece of piping, a small can of red paint tumbles out of his van, hitting the pavement and spilling out on the road.

Busted.

He bends down to pick up the paint and secures the lid, cautiously surveying his surroundings, as if he's worried someone saw him.

Oh, I saw you, Jonathan Kent. I saw you.

CHAPTER 16
SUSPECT

I sit at the kitchen table with my arms crossed, glaring at the back of Jonathan Kent's head as he fixes the broken pipe. Dad continues to drill him as he bangs away under the cabinet. It only takes him a minute to replace the piece, not giving me enough time to shake off the feeling he's the one out to get me.

Hello, red paint?

He stands up, wiping his hands on a rag, fixing his eyes on me. His blue-eyed gaze is unrelenting.

Friend or foe, Jonathan Kent?

I've met more foes lately, so the odds are stacked against you.

"You know you look like her," he says, tucking his towel into his pocket.

"Look like who?" I respond defensively.

"Anna. Your grandmother, of course," he replies with a smile.

I purse my lips. "No, I look nothing like her."

"When she was your age, dear." He chuckles. "She had the same blondish hair, although she kept hers long and straight. You have her grayish eyes. I've never known anyone to have that kind of color before. It's very rare—must be a strong Beswick trait."

"Must be."

He stands there staring at me like he's seen a ghost.

I part my lips, ready to refute him, but his phone rings, cutting me off. He pulls it from his pocket, and the sound only gets louder, escalating to ear piercing.

Old people and their ringtones. I don't get it.

He glances at the screen and then steps into the next room, his voice fading with him.

Dad's beaming with the biggest smile I've seen on him since we moved here. "How crazy is this? What are the odds of something like this happening? If I didn't know any better, Callen orchestrated this whole thing. But how could he have known?"

A little witch told him.

I shrug my shoulders and smile.

Jonathan reenters the kitchen, waving his phone at us. "I'm really enjoying my morning with you all, but business calls. A flooded basement needs my immediate attention. Once I get your water turned back on, I should go. Would it be OK if I came back sometime this week to check out the rest of the plumbing in the house? Maybe I could bring over some steaks and beers, and we could get to know each other some more. I'd really like that."

"I'd love that too. It sounds like a plan. Any night next week works for me."

"Wonderful."

The two of them pull up the calendar app on their phones. I watch as they choose the perfect date and exchange phone numbers. If I wasn't on high alert and thinking he was a suspect, this would be a beautiful moment. Once I clear him, then I'll be joyful, but for now, my guard is up.

"Hey, one more thing before I go. I wasn't going to say anything, but I think someone was tampering with my van out on the street. It might be a good idea to keep an eye on your vehicle," he says with a frown.

Dad nods in agreement. "This neighborhood isn't as safe as it was when I was a kid. Recently, someone stole Izzy's friend's Jeep while it was parked right out front."

"Is that so." Jonathan rubs his white beard.

"I hope nothing of importance was missing," Dad says.

"It's fine."

"Oh, good," Dad responds, visibly relaxing his tense shoulders.

Just wait until you see the vandalism, but then again, you could be the culprit.

"What an amazing day today turned out to be. I'm pretty sure I have a son and a granddaughter."

And I have a new suspect on my list.

JAMIE LEE FRY

CHAPTER 17
PUBLIC SAFETY

I have trust issues, and with good reason.

My first lesson in trusting the wrong person started with Sondra, which ended in death. Because of me trusting the wrong people, innocent individuals like Margo's mom and Anna have died. Megan died because I trusted Jessa would do the right thing.

But the thing I trusted the most—my gut—has failed me time and time again. Or has my gut been telling me the opposite all along, and I've failed to listen?

Right now, my gut is torn over Jonathan Kent. With everything that's happened, my radar is spinning out of whack.

I wish I had a compass to guide me to the right person.

I'm racing down the stairs to wait for Callen when he texts me that he's already outside. I skip taking a final once-over of myself in the hall tree mirror, avoiding any sort of distraction that could occur. I must remain focused on our problems at hand. I can't go and add any more to our ever-growing list.

"Bye, Dad. I'll be back later. Love you," I holler, letting the door slam behind me.

Racing down the steps, my stomach fills with unease.

Back into the lion's den I go, hi ho, hi ho.

As soon as I sink into the passenger seat of Callen's car, I'm cocooned in warmth and security. Callen's presence is like a soothing mix of lavender and sandalwood, and I can't help but feel instantly at ease with him. Who needs scented candles and essential oils when I have Callen by my side?

I take a deep breath before I spill the beans about my new grandpa. "I think Jonathan Kent did it. He painted his van. I have proof. After you drove away, a can of red paint rolled out of the back end of his van and on to the ground. He looked suspicious."

Callen huffs. "Two things to put your mind at ease. One, he's a handyman. I'm sure he has blue, green, and maybe even yellow paint stashed in his van too. Two, the Banksy wannabe could have stashed the paint in his van when he heard me coming, causing Jonathan to act suspicious, because it startled him that something was out of place." Callen holds my gaze. "Izzy, the entire world isn't bad, and Jonathan Kent isn't our villain."

"I want to agree with you. I do."

Callen rolls his eyes, knowing it's useless. Once I get something stuck in my brain, it's there until I can prove otherwise.

"So, were you able to get the gazebo graffiti covered up?" I ask.

"About that . . ." He twists away from my gaze and grips the steering wheel tightly.

My heart lurches as I wait for his response.

Spit it out.

"It got complicated. I was in the park, almost near the gazebo, when a camera crew showed up and started setting up equipment. Everything was facing the gazebo. There was no way I wouldn't get caught and accused of the destruction myself."

"Oh, crap. That's not good. What was the camera crew for?"

"I have no idea. Once I saw them, I pivoted and ran back to my car."

"Hopefully, it goes unnoticed," I respond.

"Let's hope."

"I wonder what the cameras were doing there. What if they're shooting a cool Halloween movie in our town?" I ask, trying to lighten the situation.

"I highly doubt it. That would have been huge news for our small town. And the way people gossip here, everyone would have known the second it was approved."

"Darn it. I was hoping to be an extra."

Callen laughs. "Maybe we could have been that cute couple in the background drinking coffee and staring at the trees as the main actors pass by."

"We can dream." I giggle.

"It would sure beat our reality."

"Speaking of our reality, did you prep your family?"

"Yup. They know everything. Well, the things we need them to know."

We drive the rest of the way to the Latham-Hart house in silence. Panic weaves its way through each of my organs before settling like a heavy lump in my tummy.

With trepidation, I slowly follow Callen into the kitchen, where his parents, Sid, Tahlia, and Margo, are already waiting for us. I glance around nervously, but Tim is nowhere to be seen. The atmosphere is tense, and my friend's lack of eye contact is quite apparent. The cold shoulder they're giving me is enough to make me actually shiver.

Callen pulls out a chair and gestures for me to take a seat, but I remain standing. He follows my lead and pushes the chair back in, then takes a firm stance next to me.

With everyone seated, I feel a small sense of power over them. I need the upper hand. The panic in my tummy twists and churns, but I swallow hard, keeping it at bay.

Keeping a composed expression, I begin. "Callen tells me you've all been filled in on everything. So, you know about Scarlet, the mystery girl, and the threatening images we found at the park painted on the gazebo and a vehicle outside of my house. I suppose you know about last night and the rival coven taunting us too."

Barrett gives me a dissatisfied look. Disappointing him feels like I've disappointed my own dad. He clears his throat, directing his gaze toward me and only me, pulling me further into his sphere of dissatisfaction. "Yes. We are well aware of everything you and my son have been up to."

Sid, the Latham-Hart's loyal familiar, dons a scowl that nearly rocks me from my tower of power. I slide closer to Callen to feel his calmness, hoping some of it rubs off on me.

"Well, don't you think this is cause for alarm? We're being targeted." I stomp my foot. Not that anyone can see, but it makes me feel better.

"You're being targeted," Tahlia seethes. "And you brought the target to our doorstep, Callen."

"They want Izzy," Margo adds. "What does that have to do with us?"

Sadness ripples through me.

"When there is nothing but silence in the room, don't tell me you're not hearing their chant," I respond. "It's not just me they're after. They won't rest in hell or wherever they are until they get what they want—revenge. After all, we did kill them. Wouldn't you want revenge?"

Tahlia stirs in her seat. Her gaze shifts downward, while the other witches in the room nod in agreement.

Tahlia is not hearing the chant.

Barrett remains controlled and calm, as always. "It's a residual effect of their spell. What you heard last night was the spell reminding you it's working and holding your magic hostage."

"No, it's not like that. It was sinister and real."

"I'm sure it felt real," Barrett responds.

"And what about the girl? She has to be a piece to this puzzle."

"Izzy, are you sure you aren't asking for attention?" Bree rudely suggests.

"Mom, then how do you explain the drawings?" Callen asks.

"I don't know, sweetheart. Maybe it doesn't have anything to do with us, and we're jumping to conclusions," Bree replies.

"Mom!" Callen shouts.

Bree purses her plump, red-lined lips. "I'm sorry, Callen. I just don't want the two of you seeking out problems that might not exist. We have enough on our plate without all of this."

With a sudden jolt, Tahlia springs to her feet, her phone clutched tightly in her hand.

"Riley just texted me. We need to turn on the TV. Now!" she exclaims.

His name sends shivers up and down my spine.

We all rush to the living room, following Tahlia and growing curious about what has her stirring.

Tahlia navigates the remote control, her fingers moving quickly over the buttons as she flips the TV to the local news. She rewinds the broadcast to the top of the hour, eager to catch whatever has her so worked up.

Everyone sinks into the plush, oversized couches, their eyes glued to the screen as Tahlia adjusts the volume and presses play. I remain standing in the corner, while Callen leans against the pearl-painted wall, his jaw clenched with worry. The room goes silent, except for the news anchor's voice.

"We go live to Centennial Park where mayoral candidate Joseph Dewitt is holding a press conference," the anchor says.

"So, what's the big deal?" Margo asks. "Jessa's rich jerk of a dad is on TV, so what?"

Before anyone can respond, the screen switches to Jessa's father standing behind a podium on the gazebo stairs with his wife and daughter by his side.

"Hello, good folks of East Gate. I'm honored to stand before you on this beautiful fall day as candidate for mayor of our wonderful and historic town.

"As you probably know, I'm running unopposed, and some of you might view this campaign as a formality, but I assure you, it will not be treated as such. I'm committed to serving you with the utmost dedication, and that begins today.

"I wanted to greet you all this morning with the clear vision I've outlined for the future of our quaint town, which includes a plan for historic preservation, creating more job opportunities, and an increase in public safety measures."

He pauses and his cold eyes seem to pierce through the camera lens and fixate on me, making my skin crawl.

"I come to you today with a heavy heart as we mourn the loss of a young student from our community, Megan Calhoun."

The camera flashes to a teary-eyed family, assumingly Megan's parents. I turn my attention to Margo, who's gripping the couch arm so hard it's turning her knuckles red.

"This is just one of the many tragic incidents that has left our community torn. We must stand together and take action to ensure that such incidents don't happen again. Too many of our good citizens of East Gate have died or gone missing.

"The disappearance of Norah Jamison, a local teacher, and Robin Dawson, a talented baker, has left our town unsettled and anxious for answers. The crime rate has been increasing, with instances of vandalism and car theft becoming more frequent. My own daughter's Jeep was stolen in front of the old Beswick house last month."

He mentioned my house. Ugh!

The camera scans to Jessa. She's fidgeting with her hands, twisting her fingers together, as if she's trying to calm herself down because she knows the truth, whether she wants to believe it or not.

"I vow to work tirelessly to find the answers our police force seems to have dismissed. Even today, as we were setting up our stage, my crew noticed something."

My heart falls to the pit of my stomach as the camera removes its focus on Jessa's dad and zooms in on the pentagram Callen failed to get rid of this morning.

"This town has a long, tainted, and complicated history with a blend of truth and myth. Most people would rather not remember what happened here; just think back to the tunnels outside of town in the 1800s."

I glance at Callen.

"Urban legend," Callen mouths to me.

Jessa's dad continues, "But what is known for sure is that many of its founding citizens came from Salem, Massachusetts, nearly one hundred years after the witch trials. Every few decades, something stirs within our small town, and it's chalked up to witchcraft as a joke or passing the buck. But what if it's real? This message is a threat. This person knows something, and I can't help but believe we have a coven of witches amongst our citizens."

A reporter raises his hand. "Josh Kendrick, East Gate Post." The reporter can hardly keep a straight face.

Joseph Dewitt nods.

The reporter looks him straight in the eye. "Sir, are you suggesting there are real witches in East Gate?"

"Absolutely. I believe the townsfolk of Salem were on to something, but their mission was cut short."

"Is Jessa's dad a hunter?" My quivering voice breaks the silence in the room.

"No. Joseph Dewitt is most certainly not one of us," Bree responds.

I gulp. "Do you think Jessa told him about us?"

"Jessa hardly talks to her parents. They lead separate lives unless she needs something from them. Their love is monetary," Margo responds.

"Then why is he starting a modern-day witch hunt?" I ask.

Bree grabs the remote from her daughter and flips the TV off.

"That's a good question," a familiar voice answers.

CHAPTER 18
READY TO POUNCE

Everyone's attention is drawn behind us.

Tim Hawkins steps out from the shadows like some kind of creature of the night. He's dressed in his officer uniform. "I see you caught the press conference," he remarks.

"If that's what you want to call it," Barrett says through bared teeth.

Seeing Tim makes me feel like a threatened cat; my back arched, hissing, and ready to pounce. Instead of going into full attack mode, I move closer to Callen and shrink into him.

"I had a heads-up that part of that speech was coming. Joseph Dewitt spent the better part of yesterday on a heated rant with the Chief of Police. I overheard most of it. It was hard not to.

"Joseph blames the police department for their laziness in the Calhoun case and for letting Sam off the hook. He won't let up about the missing women, either. He even approached me, inquiring about Mia's unexpected vanishing act, but I gave him nothing."

Tears spill down Margo's face at the mention of her mother. I want to console her, but I'm afraid to move.

"And don't get me started about his daughter's car. He won't shut up about the darn thing. But what I wasn't expecting was that bit about the witches. He's off the rails and needs to be stopped," Tim adds.

Barrett strokes his chin. "We were surprised Joseph took that approach too. He's always been a bullheaded man who easily got sucked into folklore and gossip, but this is a whole new level. Couldn't he just take office and do nothing like our last mayor?"

That explains Jessa's obsession with my Gran-gran. Her dad was feeding her stories and tales.

"If the witches are found out, it won't be long before the hunters are too. That's why I'm here. Does this have anything to do with—" Tim nods his head to me.

I can feel his hatred creeping over my shoulders and wrapping around me like a boa constrictor, squeezing the life out of me.

Barrett crosses the room, putting himself between Tim and me. "No, no—I doubt it has anything to do with any of us," he says, making it obvious he's trying to protect me.

Despite the fact that we're all working together to solve our many issues, it's clear I'm still a sore spot for Tim—the one who got away. His eyes narrow as they meet mine, a dark, cold storm brewing beneath the surface.

"Let's take this into the kitchen, and we can chat over a fresh pot of coffee," Barrett offers.

Tim's eyes gleam with a mischievous glint that turns my

body into ice. I go still as a statue, afraid to move, for the hunter seems to be on the prowl.

What's with the Hawkins' men? Can't they be more like Bree?

Thankfully, he turns his head. As soon as he's out of my sight, I hurry down the long grandeur hallway. I'm desperate to take refuge in Callen's bedroom, the weight of my worries pressing down on me, nearly suffocating me. Everything in my mind is a jumbled mess. My emotions are spiraling out of control, and I can't seem to catch my breath.

Callen notices my distress and catches up with me in the middle of the long hallway. He pushes on the door to the left of the guest room, where I witnessed Anna succumbing to flames. I hurry inside with my heart racing. Callen is quick to follow with his hand on the doorknob, ready to lock it behind us, shutting out the world and Tim Hawkins.

I take a deep breath, feeling the tension start to melt away. I'm safe with Callen—at least for now.

CHAPTER 19
DRIVING ME CRAZY

"Everything is falling apart." I try to catch my breath, but a sob catches in my throat, making it nearly impossible to calm down.

"We'll be discovered and burned at the stake or hung by a jury of our friends and peers. The Beswick girl will be the first to go. Bring on the gallows." My chest heaves with each word.

Callen calmly grabs my wrists and stands tall, his voice barely above a whisper. "Take a deep breath, Beswick."

His request seems impossible, but I slowly follow his lead. With each inhale and exhale, my body relaxes and my mind begins to clear. I finally see what's in front of me.

It's Callen; it's always been Callen.

He's my rock.

He's the one.

He's not a hunter.

I melt, pressing myself into his chest, folding into the effortlessness of being with him.

He pulls back and gently cups my face with his hands. He gazes intently into my eyes, making the world around us fade into insignificance. "Izzy," he says with bated breath.

"Callen," I whimper, my insides quivering.

His muscles tense and flex against my chest. With each breath, our hearts beat together as one. He reaches out and grabs a piece of my hair, twirling it around his finger, keeping his velvety eyes locked intently on mine.

"Please tell me you feel what I feel?" he softly asks.

I shake my head, trying to suppress the words that threaten to spill out of my mouth—my usual response layered with guilt. But when I open my mouth, the words don't come. There is no guilt. Riley stirred up emotions in me, but this moment with Callen is on a completely different level. Every doubt and every uncertainty is gone—faded away. Everything is clear now.

It's me and Callen. It's always been us.

"I've wanted to kiss you since the day I met you, Izzy Beswick." He grins wildly at me, dragging his finger across the outline of my lips.

My cheeks grow warm from his touch.

"May I finally kiss you?"

I nod my head slowly. My lips part open on their own accord, as if drawn open by some invisible force. The moment our lips touch, a tingle ignites in my chest, sending a frenzy throughout my body that I can't ignore. I lean further into him, our bodies melding together as we spill over onto the bed as one.

Keeping his eyes on mine, Callen twists his head ever so slightly. "Are you sure this is what you want—that I'm what you want?"

"Yes," I respond wholeheartedly.

He drags his lips down my neck, sweetly kissing every inch of my exposed skin. My lips quiver, longing for his lips to meet mine again.

"I've never felt like this before—with anyone. You're special, Izzy. We belong together."

He wraps his arms around me, pulling me closer to him. My body bursts with desire. I want Callen. I want all of him.

As we lay on his satiny, king-sized bed, our faces inches apart, his hand gently brushes my hair away from my eyes. He kisses the tip of my nose. "You're driving me crazy, Beswick," he says, his inky eyes locked with mine.

My heart thrashes wildly against my chest, sending waves of adrenaline through my veins, my mind racing with the possibilities of what's coming.

But instead of leaning back in for another kiss, he pulls away from me as if something has changed.

My heart sinks, and I can't help but whimper, "Why did you stop?"

He pauses for a moment, biting his lower lip as if considering his words carefully. "We can't let things get too carried away—not yet," he finally replies. "After your birthday."

A tinge of disappointment shoots through me like an electric shock. "December can't come soon enough," I whisper, reaching out for his hand.

Through a strained smile, he says, "You're telling me."

"We're not even a full year apart in age," I pout, ready to feel something more.

"Gosh, you're so darn beautiful, even when you pout. But eighteen is still eighteen." His gaze drops to the bedding as he scrunches up a handful of sheets in his fist. "And I'm eighteen and you're not."

"But we can still make out, right?" I playfully ask.

In one swift motion, he reaches out and pulls me toward him, wrapping his arms around me and securing me against his chest. As we sit there on his bed, our gazes lock. "You read my mind, Beswick—kindred spirits."

CHAPTER 20
PRIVATE

I bask in the warmth of Callen's bed, enveloped in his soft satin sheets, my body partially exposed. I shift my gaze around the room, and my eyes are drawn to a stunning green leather-bound book nestled in the partially open drawer of his nightstand. The book beckons to me, urging me to reach out and grab it.

I glance over at Callen, who's fallen asleep. So, I get out of bed and take the book to his desk in the corner of the room.

My heart races as I ponder whether I'm intruding on his privacy. But curiosity gets the better of me, and I can't resist the temptation. I open the cover, careful not to crease the perfect spine as it appears he's taken good care of his book.

This Book of Shadows belongs to Callen Latham-Hart.

His penmanship is striking. He must have used a quill and ink; the words are rich and velvety and flow seamlessly across the heavy paper. I feel like I'm discovering something new about the boy I just spent hours kissing. It's hard to imagine him hunched over this desk, quill in hand, carefully dipping it into the inkwell. It doesn't seem like the Callen I know. But it does put my spellwork to shame. I'm almost embarrassed by the crumpled sheet of paper I handed him last night.

Reaching for the corner to carefully turn the heavily weighted paper, I notice the edges are gilded in gold, giving the journal a touch of luxury.

Must be nice to be a Latham-Hart.

As I flip the pages, each spell in his collection seems to be meticulously crafted with precise instructions. He even includes the ideal moon phase for the spell to be performed and which candle and element aid the best result.

Callen is more knowledgeable than he let on.

He sure has an impressive array of spells for someone who only discovered he was a true witch a year ago. As I flip the pages, skimming through the large book, my eyes catch on the glamour spell and the spell he cunningly used to frame Sam Hornsby—it's all there.

A strange sensation flutters in my stomach, causing me to pause.

Without warning, Callen's voice creeps up from behind me. "Is that my book of shadows?" he asks, his tone defensive.

I hastily shut the book. "Y-yes," I stutter. "I'm sorry. I was curious."

"Izzy, that's private," he snaps.

"But I thought—"

"You thought wrong." Callen snatches the book from my hands, but it slips from his grip.

Pages flutter wildly, flapping in the air as the beautiful leather-bound journal lands on its spine wide open.

His eyes grow wide with panic as we both react and reach for it, but he's too late. I see what has him so upset. I see what he's trying to hide.

A Lover's Connection Spell.

CHAPTER 21
LESSONS IN TRUST

A Lover's Connection Spell

Hail to the guardians of earth, air, fire, and water.
Beloved goddess of love, I ask for your help from above.
I feel her presence in the air.
I know she is rare.
We have a connection.
Give her a little push in my direction.
With a loving mind and loving heart, make it so we never part.
Foster this connection,
For she is perfection.
Let our thoughts become one,
From this moment on.
So shall it be.

The room starts to spin, leaving me disoriented, confused, and gasping for air. Everything's closing in on me. I struggle to keep my bearings and search for something to ground me, but nothing seems to catch. Instead, my eyes are drawn to Callen's homemade altar on the other side of the room. An array of colorful candles adorns his setup. One candle in particular jumps out at me as if it's been screaming at me, waiting for me to see it—the pink candle from Invoke Awakenings.

Pink is for love.

My eyes fall back to the book, and further instructions are inscribed near the bottom of the page in Callen's perfect handwriting.

Moon phase: Waxing Moon
Candle: Pink
Elements: Water and Fire

No! No! No!

Hot tears stream uncontrollably down my face, and it feels like my heart is being ripped from my chest. "You put a spell on me? To what? Make me fall in love with you?" I ask, my voice trembling with hurt and anger.

Callen remains still, offering no response.

I let out a scream, feeling the weight of his betrayal crushing me. "Our entire relationship is a lie." I drop to the ground, curling into a protective ball. "How could you, Callen? I'm so foolish for believing in a connection that was never real."

"Izzy." He reaches his arm out, but I swat it away.

"Don't touch me," I hiss.

"I never used the spell. I didn't have to," Callen responds.

"You're a liar. How can I ever believe anything that comes

out of your mouth again? How do I know anything you've said to me is real?"

"You were never meant to see that spell."

"Well, I did," I snap.

He drops down to the carpet and wraps his arms around me.

"No," I push him away. "You don't get to do that. Everything was a lie."

His face droops. "It's not like that."

A wave of nausea washes over me. I curl back into a ball, hugging my legs tightly, trying to block everything out, including Callen.

I close my eyes and try to remember my home before I moved here, with the calming noises of the Puget Sound behind my house, the cooing seagulls, and the feisty waves crashing into the shore. It gives me a brief respite from this nightmare, from Callen and his lies.

But now everything is messed up—gone down the crapper, as Dad used to say.

Anger wraps its way through my body, propelling me to my feet. "Whatever this was—it was a mistake. I never want to talk to you again."

"Izzy, wait!" Callen reaches for me, but I storm out of his bedroom, slamming the door behind me, desperate to escape the pain on the other side.

I need to get out of the Latham-Hart house once and for all. No one wants me here. I'm better off on my own— alone, where no one can hurt me.

I pivot in a hurry and collide with someone in the darkness

of the long hallway. Afraid to make eye contact in fear it's one of the hunters in the house, I try to dodge them, but a soft hand pulls me back.

Through the blur of my tears, Margo's features slowly come into focus, her reddish-brown curls bouncing around her face as if still in motion.

"What's wrong?" she asks with concern.

I stammer out a few words, struggling to form a coherent sentence. "Cal-Callen." Tears slide down my face, catching on my chin.

Margo nods, her eyes filling with empathy instead of the meanness she's come at me with lately. "Come on," she says, taking my hand in hers. "Let's go talk about it."

Without uttering another word, she leads me into the nearest bathroom, which happens to be the second to the last door, just before the eerie entrance to the basement lair of secrets.

I shudder, thinking about the cage that's probably right below my feet.

"What happened?" she gently asks.

I drop to the floor, feeling the coldness of the porcelain tiles seeping through my jeans. A shiver works its way up my backside.

Could it be any colder in here?

Margo flips a switch as if reading my mind, and the tiles grow warm under me, filling me with a much-needed sense of comfort.

Of course, they have heated floors.

Margo smiles and takes a seat next to me.

I take a deep breath, gathering my thoughts, before I ask the question gnawing at me. "Why are you being so nice to me?"

She stares at me with a mixture of sadness, empathy, and something else I can't quite put my finger on—perhaps it's curiosity. "I don't know, but I can't let you leave like this, so go on." She nods for me to continue. "Are you going to spill the beans or not? What happened?"

I let out a deep sigh. "I don't know where to start. Everything is so messed up."

I hesitate, waiting for her to continue coaxing it out of me, but she doesn't say another word, so I let the words spew out of my mouth like word vomit. "I found Callen's book of shadows. He crafted a lover's spell to ensure we'd be connected—well, connected more than a witch's connection should be. Our entire friendship was built on a lie."

Confusion sweeps over my beautiful, sweet friend's features, resting heavily on her forehead in the form of a sharp crease.

It's confession time.

"Margo, you know how sometimes we could feel each other's emotions, like that day in the attic?"

She nods.

"And remember the day we went into the forest when you saw my thoughts? Did you ever wonder how that happened?"

"I try not to think about it," she solemnly replies, tears slipping down her round face.

"I've been keeping a secret," I confess with shame punishing my insides. "I've been trying to keep our connection a secret. I didn't want you to know how connected we truly are—well, were."

"OK," she responds cautiously.

"Trust me, it was for your own good. I didn't want you to see Megan's death through my eyes. That's why I pulled away from you that day in the forest. You didn't need to see the whole thing. I knew if you saw us there, hearing the whole conversation, it would have been too hard and painful." My heart aches for Margo as I say the words out loud.

She eyes me curiously, her lips pursing into a flat line. "Keep going."

"Callen and I have—well, had, the same connection, but it was one hundred times stronger. He didn't have to touch me or even be near me to read my thoughts. I thought that made us special. We called it kindred spirits. He made me believe we were meant for each other. But it was all a lie. He used a spell to ensure we'd be connected."

Margo gasps. "That rat."

I smile, happy to hear she's on my side.

"He pushed me away from Riley and made me fall for him instead, but it was all based on a lie. He made me believe we were soulmates and made me feel guilty for choosing to be with Riley over him. He used magic to control the Megan situation, and in turn, control me by using it as a bonded connection of secrets based on lies."

A single tear escapes from the corner of Margo's eye and rolls down her cheek.

"I'm sorry. I didn't mean to upset you again. My problems are nothing compared to what you're going through. I'm sorry. I can go." I attempt to stand up, but Margo quickly pulls me back, her grip firm yet gentle.

"No, it's OK. This is good. We need to be honest and talk, like really talk," she says with a small smile.

"Margo, I'm so sorry for everything. I didn't kill Megan, but I feel awful about how she died. I'm sorry I kept our connection hidden from you."

"I know you didn't physically run her over. Jessa did that. But you could have made Jessa stop."

"Margo, you were passed out, but I'm not sure you would have made the right choice had you been awake."

"You might be right," she concedes, her gaze falling to her fidgeting hands.

"I truly thought I was doing the right thing."

Margo sighs and slides closer to me, both of us now leaning against the bathroom vanity side by side.

"And about your mom . . . I had no idea she was summoned by the rival coven. I didn't even know who she was until it was too late. I know me being here, being the chosen one that everyone is out to get, put everyone else in danger, but I didn't choose this. I didn't even want you girls in my house if I'm being totally honest. Jessa bullied me into it, and things took a life of their own from that point on. I was only doing what I thought was right."

"I can't forgive you, Izzy, but I can start to understand," Margo says, her eyes full of tears.

"I don't want to fight anymore," I say softly.

She nods. "Me neither."

"I made a mistake."

"You made a lot of mistakes, sweetie." She leans in and rests her head on my shoulder.

"I missed you," I say, my voice breaking with each word.

"I missed you too," Margo responds sweetly.

"So, what are we going to do about the witch hunt?" Margo asks, wiping away her tears. "I can't believe Jessa's dad."

"We'll figure it out," I say, determined to protect my friends. This time, I won't fail.

"This is all so crazy. Who would have thought something like this would happen? I mean, give us a gosh darn break, and let us catch our breath, you know?" Margo says.

"I can't believe Jessa isn't trying to reason with her dad. She knows what's at stake—her friend's lives. Can't she tell him to cool it with the witch talk?"

"Her *ex-friend's* lives," Margo corrects me. "And you haven't met Jessa's dad. There's no telling that man anything. But enough about Jessa and her asshole parents."

Margo's eyes mischievously sparkle as she turns her gaze to me. "Now, are you going to give me the details about Callen? I know he was a jerk, but did you kiss him?"

My cheeks glow with embarrassment. "I did," I admit, biting my bottom lip, suddenly feeling shy.

"How was it?" Margo probes.

"It was perfect before I found out his secret," I reply, feeling a pang of regret.

"I can't believe you kissed Callen." Margo covers her eyes with her hands and squeals at my news.

Before I can respond, the door creaks open and Tahlia startles us, her eyes narrowing with anger, the colors within them shifting and changing like a kaleidoscope.

Hunter eyes.

"You kissed my brother!" she exclaims.

Silence seizes me. I don't know how to respond.

Tahlia's wild eyes pin on me. "I can't believe you did that to Riley."

"Did what to Riley?" A voice booms from behind her, causing my heart to race with panic.

CHAPTER 22
LESSONS IN CONTROL

Riley's voice knocks the wind from me, and the air turns cold, causing the hairs on the back of my neck to stand on end.

Time seems to stop as my ex-boyfriend slowly emerges from the darkness and into the harsh bathroom light. Shadows cling to him like a cloak, while his hate-filled eyes swirl wildly with a vortex of emotion. His face is a mask of fury, with his furrowed brows and tense jawline. It's as if every fiber of his being is focused on his desire to drain the life out of me.

My heart pounds in my chest, and I swear I can feel the color draining from my face. I try to move, but my body's heavy and unresponsive. Fear has taken a hold of me, and I'm unable to break free from its grip. My lungs constrict, allowing very few words to trickle out. "Wh-what is he doing here?"

Tahlia's eyes flash to me. "Don't worry about that." Her words hiss like a snake ready to strike.

The change is coming.

Riley's muscles bulge beneath his shirt, and his fists are

clenched tightly at his sides. It's clear he's struggling to control his urges.

Move over, lions; I'm in the hunter's den now.

"You did *what* to Riley?" Riley presses again. The tension in his words is evident. He takes a step into the room, towering over us, making me feel small and powerless.

I try to speak, but my words get stuck in my throat.

"Come on, Riley. Not now." Margo tries to intervene, but Riley dismisses her.

His focus remains solely on me. His piercing gaze is almost unbearable, as if it's burning a hole through my soul. As he stares at me, his eyes change color, turning into a blazing shade of red I've never seen before. The sight of it only fuels the fear that's already coursing through my veins. A million different lies race through my mind. I can't upset the hunter inside of him. Revealing the truth would only make it worse.

Riley's words circle in my head like a merry-go-round. *I wanted you to die. I wanted you to die. I wanted you to die.*

I know I should keep my mouth shut, and every fiber of my being is screaming for me to run.

"I'm waiting, Izzy." Riley taps his foot aggressively against the porcelain tiles. He tilts his head, his nostrils flaring.

"What does it matter?"

Did I say that out loud?

"Izzy kissed Callen," Tahlia blurts out.

Gee, thanks, Tahlia.

Riley's upper lip curls into a sneer. "How could you do that to me?"

Is he joking?

I wanted you to die. I wanted you to die. I wanted you to die. The merry-go-round continues at warp speed. *I wanted you to die.*

"Are you kidding me right now? You aren't my boyfriend. You said it yourself that you wanted me to die." The instant the words slip from my mouth, I regret it. I'm trapped and there's nowhere to run.

A myriad of emotions flicker across his face; first anger, then irritation, followed by confusion.

I tense, waiting for the hunter side to unleash its terror on me. His eyes finally flicker with the predatory glint I'm expecting. I grit my teeth and brace for what's to come. But to my surprise, he shifts his feet and without saying a word, storms out of the room.

What the heck was that?

"Riley," I call out, unsure why I'm even trying.

He doesn't come back.

I spring to my feet and shove past Tahlia, who's standing in my way. "Thanks a lot," I snap, pushing her into the doorframe.

Tahlia winces, and I instantly feel guilty for my rage, but my mind is too clouded with confusion to apologize.

I catch a glimpse of Riley sprinting down the hallway. Without a second thought, I run after him.

Stupid girl, what are you doing?

Turn around.

Once he's out of the long hallway, I expect him to take the stairs to Tahlia's room, but he surprises me by passing through the living room and rushing through the front door.

Without hesitation, I continue to run after him.

Stupid girl, turn around.

As I pass by Tim, Sid, Bree, and Barrett, their curious gazes lock onto mine, but I don't stop to explain. I continue to chase Riley.

"Riley!" I shout, shooting through the front door.

"Stay away from me," he urges from the bottom of the driveway.

"Can we at least try to talk?" I plead.

Riley darts forward, but manages to stop himself. "You're not safe near me," he shouts, his voice pained.

"I know, but you owe me an explanation."

"No, I think you're the one who owes the explanation, Izzy."

Even from a distance, I can see he's gritting his teeth, and his hands are twitching at his sides.

"What do you mean?" I ask.

"Why didn't you respond to my message yesterday?"

"I didn't see the need to after you said you wanted me to die."

His face contorts in pain. "Is that the only thing you took from that whole text?"

My body involuntarily curls forward, and my eyes drift downward, avoiding his eye contact. "I didn't actually see the whole message; I accidentally deleted the text."

"Seriously, Izzy," Riley says. He pulls his phone from his pocket. "I'm resending it now."

I stare at my phone, waiting for his text to come through.

As I wait, I ask, "Can I ask what you're doing here? Isn't

it hard to be in a house full of witches?"

The sound of approaching footsteps sneaks up on me. I turn to see Margo and Tahlia standing behind me.

Margo swiftly moves past me, positioning herself in the massive space between Riley and me.

"Yes, that's why I'm here," Riley responds.

My face scrunches up in confusion.

Margo's gaze shifts to Riley. "Riley, you won't hurt her."

Riley winces and takes a hesitant step closer, his face etched with pain. "Bree is trying to help me manage my emotions when I'm around witches. Margo and Barrett—"

"Are bait," Margo cuts him off. "Izzy, Riley hasn't attacked me. He's learning to control the hunter side, just like Bree."

"But he attacked Callen yesterday in the park," I divulge.

"Watching the two of you together, I couldn't help but be consumed by jealousy. But it wasn't because of my hunter side, Izzy. It's because I still care about you. That's all that was." His face flushes. "Has that darn message come through yet?"

I glance to my phone, and there it is waiting for me.

One new message from Riley.

Riley: Izzy, I've been keeping my distance and it's given me a new sense of clarity.

That day in the forest I WANTED YOU TO DIE. Typing those words makes me sick. I hate to admit that.

When I dropped that dagger, part of me wanted to see what our teacher would do to you. With that awful thought running through my mind, I knew it wasn't safe for you to be around me anymore. The hate that ran through my veins wasn't me.

I think you were right about my wires getting crossed because I didn't feel like that toward Margo when they directed me to kill her. I didn't have the same thirst for her as I did you. I assume my love for you was warped into a revengeful desire to kill you.

I hope you know I don't want to feel like this, but it's hard to ignore. Maybe someday we can make things work. I'll keep trying, Izzy.

Love always, Riley <3

My already broken heart splinters into even smaller pieces, slicing my insides to shreds as it slides into the pit of my stomach.

I royally fucked up.

CHAPTER 23
I HAVE A SOUL

I really messed up. All this while, I accused Riley of abandoning me, but it turns out he was doing exactly what I wanted him to do. The realization hits me like a ton of bricks, and I feel sick to my stomach. I trusted the wrong person.

I stare at Riley, struggling to find the right words. "I'm sorry," is all I manage to say.

"I understand. Things are very confusing right now," he replies in a sympathetic tone, while his eyes swirl wildly, suggesting otherwise.

"You can say that again," I say, my voice shaking.

He frowns.

Taking a deep breath, I prepare myself for my next question. "I need to ask you something, and I hope you won't hate me for it. Did you leave a drawing on the gazebo and another on a van parked outside my house this morning?" I ask, trying to keep my voice steady.

"What kind of drawing?" His eyes narrow as he tries to figure out what I'm getting at. "Wait, are you talking about the one Jessa's dad pointed out on TV?"

Margo's curious gaze meets mine as I shake my head. I don't have to turn around to know Tahlia's standing tensely behind me.

"Yeah, Hawkins, was it you?" Callen appears in the doorway, making my skin crawl at the sight of him.

Riley huffs. "I know I have hunter blood coursing through my veins, but I'm still human, and I have a soul. I wouldn't put everyone in danger, let alone threaten anyone. I don't want to be a hunter. I don't want to feel like this."

"Callen, please go inside. I've got this handled," I say firmly, wanting to avoid any further confrontation or a repeat of last night. Both boys are sporting bruised faces as it is.

"It seems you've let your guard down around hunter boy," Callen sneers.

"No, Callen, I've let my guard down around you."

"So, you two are a thing now?" Riley hisses.

"No," I quickly respond.

Before anyone else can say anything, Bree's voice carries from inside the house. "Kids, get inside now. There's something you need to see. Hurry."

"Mom, what's happening?" Tahlia spins around and rushes inside.

Bree doesn't answer her daughter's question. Instead, she leads the way through the long hallway that oozes grandness.

We follow the graceful huntress into the spacious office at the end of the hallway, this time with less curiosity, but still the same amount of fear.

Bree presses her hand on the left side of the vacant wall, and I can't help but notice Riley's reluctance to stand near me. Instead, he looms nervously in the doorway. Callen, on the other hand, positions himself boldly between us, still attempting to play the hero.

The partition slides open with a creak, revealing the ominous staircase leading to the basement of secrets. My palms get clammy as we file down the steps two by two, Margo's grip on my arm tightening with each step. The air grows colder the deeper we descend.

Bree pauses at the final door, giving it a knock. "Everyone's here," she says.

Sid opens the door, and we all walk into the basement, our eyes scanning the room with apprehension.

What are we walking into?

CHAPTER 24
GLOWING

My heart races and I feel as though I'm trapped in a nightmare I can't escape from. The urge to let out a scream and run away is almost overwhelming. However, I know I need to stay and see what has the adults on high alert. I hoped I'd never be in this room again, especially with three—maybe four—hunters.

My eyes fall to Barrett and Tim standing inside the cage; it's quite the sight. The tension exuding from them sends my nerves into a frenzy. But it's what lies on the thick wooden table in front of them that captures my attention—the necklaces.

"Watch this," Tim says, stepping away from the table.

An eerie glow emanates from the necklace on the far end of the table, casting an ominous aura around the room.

"Now, watch," Tim says, stepping back into the cage.

The glow slowly fades until it's nonexistent.

Tim steps away again, and the glow resumes, even brighter than the first time. He walks over to Margo and whispers in her ear. Margo nods and slowly enters the cage, the color draining in her face. She stands before the table and hovers her hand over the necklaces.

"This one is mine. I'm sure of it." Margo points at the third one in the lineup and then joins Barrett behind the table.

The third necklace glows with a mystical light as if on command.

I enter the jail cell, fearing it's a hunter's trap, but curiosity overcomes my fear. As I step closer, the fourth necklace lights up as if in response to my presence, filling the room with a warm, golden glow.

Callen takes a deep breath, his eyes fixed on the fifth necklace. "Here goes nothing," he mutters, his hand hovering over the ancient item.

The pendant begins to glow with a faint purple light.

"Come here, Tahlia," Barrett beckons to his daughter, gesturing for her to join them.

Tahlia steps forward, her eyes fixed on the remaining necklace. Nothing happens.

"Maybe you should pick it up," Barrett suggests.

She reaches for it, her fingers closing around the large purple and black pendant.

I gasp, but quickly cover my mouth.

The necklace remains dark and lifeless, refusing to respond to her touch.

"What if you try holding it tighter?" Barrett suggests.

Tahlia's mossy green eyes fixate on the necklace with intense concentration. But no matter how tightly Tahlia grips the magical item, it remains stubbornly unresponsive, leaving everyone puzzled.

"Maybe this one's not yours," I say, causing everyone to look at me with confusion.

"What I mean is that there's another necklace out there. Remember the one from my dad's hospital room? The one I told the nurse to dispose of."

"Oh my goodness, that's right," Callen says. "I bet that one belongs to you, T."

"Then who does this one belong to and why?"

Tim grits his teeth and says, "It's Steven's."

"No," I respond.

Barrett turns to me. "Izzy, I think it's time we talk to your dad. I don't know why these necklaces are calling to us, but I believe we all need to be together to restore our magic, and that includes your dad. You must tell me everything you remember about that nurse. Then Tim and I will work to track her down. Once we have the final necklace, it will be time to talk to your dad."

"So, you think there's hope for us?" Margo asks.

Barrett glides his hand over the necklaces, four out of five of them glowing in hope. "This is magic."

CHAPTER 25
TILT-A-WHIRL

Standing outside the Latham-Hart estate, I take a deep breath of the crisp, fresh autumn air, filling my lungs to full capacity. Finally, I can breathe again after what felt like hours of holding my breath. I'm grateful to be free from that suffocating house and on my way home. Although, I should have accepted Barrett's offer to give me a ride. I'm not in the mood to walk, but at least it's mostly downhill. I couldn't bear the look of disappointment on Barrett's face a second longer after I told him everything I could remember about the intensive care unit nurse and the stupid fact that I told her I didn't care what she did with the necklace.

A moment alone might not be a bad thing, though. I have a lot to process and unpack emotionally. It's been a day.

As I wander down the driveway, feeling almost free, my phone annoyingly vibrates. I don't need magical powers to know who's texting me. The urge to ignore it is strong, but I give in and check it anyway.

Callen: Izzy, don't walk home. Please let me drive you so we can talk. I want to explain.

That's a big fat nope.

I slip my phone into my pocket, ignoring Callen and his desperate plea for my attention. Tucking my chin down, I brace for the wind stirring up around me. As I walk, I immerse myself in my own little world of worries, attempting to unravel the chaos of the day. Every question nags at me, fighting for my immediate attention. Are Margo and I OK now? Did my little bathroom confession bring us back together? Can we really trust the necklaces that so freely lit up before our very eyes, calling to each witch, except Tahlia? Could the missing pendant really be hers, or is she turning into a hunter like Riley? Suppose we don't get our magic back before her birthday; could she be lost to the dark side for good?

The nagging questions continue in the form of a never-ending spiral of maddening thoughts, swirling around like a tilt-a-whirl, causing waves of nausea to wash over me. Can Riley really be trained to be around me without his predestined hate taking the front seat? And even if he can, does it change anything? It's sweet that he's trying, but if I'm being honest with myself, my heart didn't leap with joy; it still lurched with guilt.

And then there's Callen, which is a whole heaping pile of fucked up. I can't hide the fact that everything felt perfect lying in his warm bed, wrapped in his embrace, but he messed up when he personally designed the path of our relationship. Will I ever trust him again?

As the leaves crunch under my feet, my thoughts shift to my dad, the final spin of the tilt-a-whirl, the twirl that is make or break if I'm going to be sick, and all signs are pointing to yes.

Can I really tell my dad the truth?

If I do, how will he react? Will he be mad at me for keeping this from him for months, or will he be angry at his family for failing to tell him the truth? Will he blame Anna's death on me?

I shiver as another breeze whips past me, this time chilling me to the bone. But maybe it's not the weather that's turned me ice cold; it's all the things I must face.

My phone vibrates again.

Ugh. You got to be kidding me.

Callen: I wish you wouldn't have left. We need to talk. Izzy, please don't ignore me.

I shouldn't respond, but my fingers are already angrily typing out a response.

Izzy: No, we don't need to talk! You betrayed my trust, and that's all I need to know.

Callen: Please come back.

Izzy: No. I have a lot to think about. Please just leave me alone.

As I put my phone away for a second time, my gaze is drawn toward a nearby birch tree as if pulled by some inexplicable force. My heart sinks as I notice the same pentagram from before has been carved into the white bark, accompanied this time by a message written in bold, red letters: *I KNOW THE TRUTH*

My fingers move with lightning speed as I grab my phone and snap a picture. I'm about to send it to everyone, but my eyes catch on something in the background. I pinch the screen to zoom in, and I'm hit with honey-brown hair swaying in the wind—Scarlet.

Oh, you're so busted.

I sprint after her, my lungs working furiously to keep up, releasing ragged gasps. My feet pound against the pavement, growing heavier with each stride as I zig-zag through yards and down unfamiliar side streets. I pause to catch my breath in front of a stunning historic home, knowing I've lost sight of her, but I swear still sense her presence in the air.

What is it with this girl?

Fueled by my yearning to uncover the truth, I resume my pace, uncertain of my direction. I'm not entirely surprised when I end up at my house and the entrance to the forest.

Of course she led me here.

Although I'm blinded to her whereabouts, a powerful force tugs at me, urging me to continue. The pull is so strong that I dash into the trees without a second thought. Sprinting into the dense forest, my heart pounds, and my body aches. With every step, the pull grows stronger. I don't know where I'm going, but I know I'm going somewhere important. I feel it in my bones.

I come to a screeching halt when I approach an old, run-down structure nestled discreetly in ivy and twisted trees.

As I draw closer, my footsteps are cautious. It's as if the decrepit building is beckoning me closer, and I can't resist its pull.

The structure is small and crooked, with a thatched roof that looks like it could cave in at any moment. Could this be the very fort where Isobel and my dad used to spend time, testing his magic away from Anna's watchful eyes? My dad talked about it on our drive moving out here, and Isobel mentioned it in her diary, but this isn't what I imagined. This isn't what normal people would call a fort. It's more like a cottage.

With a rush of adrenaline, I turn the rusty doorknob. As the door creaks open, I'm hit with a musty smell, but it's clear someone is living here.

"Found you, Scarlet."

CHAPTER 26
CHASING GHOSTS

My heart races with anticipation as my gaze meticulously searches every inch of the so-called fort, hoping to find any clue that could reveal Scarlet's true identity. But so far, no Scarlet.

I'm hesitant to go inside, but I have no other options, and time isn't on my side. The setting sun is urging me to leave, but I ignore it, taking the first step anyway.

As I enter, a cloud of dust rises from the floor, and sticky cobwebs greet me at every turn. They sway effortlessly with the breeze that seeps through every crack and crevice in the weathered walls. Light filters its way through the cracks and casts long, eerie shadows that dance along the rotting floorboards.

"Hello. I know you're close. You led me here, but why? I just want to talk. I want to know why you're threatening and following me," I call out, hoping for a response.

But there is no answer, only the creaking of the structure swaying with the ever-growing wind. It howls through the room, stirring up even more dust, making me cough several times.

I continue my search, shouting Scarlet's name into the emptiness of the one-room cottage. My eyes scan every corner, every crevice, but there is no sign of her except for a lone blanket on the floor, a half-burnt candle, and a cup filled with water. These items are my only evidence that she's real and not a figment of my imagination.

I drop down beside her simple bed, feeling defeated and questioning my sanity. I'm the only one who's seen her. Maybe there is no Scarlet at all, and I'm chasing a ghost.

But then, as everything seems lost, I notice words written in the dust: *Nothing is as it seems.*

"Nothing is as it seems," I say the words out loud as the last bit of light fades into nothingness.

I need to go.

CHAPTER 27
SCARLET'S SOUNDTRACK

I dash through the dense forest, my feet trampling on the crisp leaves that crunch beneath my Converse sneakers. My heart thumps wildly in my chest as I try to remember the path I took earlier. The last thing I need is to get lost in these creepy old woods. Everything looks different now that the sun has dipped behind the trees.

Every rustle of the leaves and every twig snap makes me jump. I can't shake the haunting feeling that Scarlet's out there lurking in the darkness and watching my every move.

I pull out my phone and use the flashlight to help navigate my way, hoping to avoid all the tree roots and hidden rocks nestled into the ground, waiting for me to make a misstep.

As I quicken my pace, the wind whistles through the trees, creating an eerie melody that reverberates through the forest. The sound is so haunting and imprints in my memory, much like the soothing sounds of the Puget Sound that have found a permanent place in my mind. The effect of the howling wind is the polar opposite, though. It's as if the breeze is playing a soundtrack for Scarlet—the mystery girl—and this creepy tune would be the number one track on her album.

With each step I take, the cold of the night creeps up my back like the ghosts of those who died in the forest, attaching itself to my soul. I shake the feeling away and keep moving, determined to make it out of the woods and to my home safely.

I'm relieved when the soft, comforting light from my house comes into focus through the trees. It's calling out to me like a beacon in the night.

As I approach my house, my phone notifies me that my battery has dwindled down to five percent, and the flashlight turns off. I couldn't have planned this any better. For once, something worked out for me.

Taking the final steps to the back porch, my phone buzzes with several messages, one after another.

Callen: 3 new messages.

Barrett: 2 new messages.

I decide Callen's messages can wait, opening Barrett's text thread first.

Barrett: The nurse was a dead end.

"There goes the start of things working out," I say to an empty porch.

Barrett: She kept the necklace, but she said it was stolen a couple of days ago.

Izzy: That's convenient. Do you believe her?

Barrett: I do. She was upset about it. Plus, I had Tim with me, and the badge always helps people tell the truth. She told us she felt bad keeping it, but didn't know what else to do with it. She was very upset that it went missing. She had grown attached to the necklace and was about to have it appraised. She thought it was worth something.

Izzy: It's worth something all right!

As I wait for Barrett's response, I question if I should tell everyone about Scarlet. I didn't have time to send the picture I took earlier. Maybe this is one thing I should keep to myself until I know more.

Nothing is as it seems.

The vibration from my phone rocks me from my thoughts, pulling my attention back to my conversation. I can check the fort each day. Something tells me she has nowhere to go, so she'll be back. I hope.

Barrett: Tim had her file a police report, so at least we can keep looking into it. Not much we can do until something comes up. Keep your eyes and ears open.

Izzy: OK. I will.

Barrett: Izzy, I think it's time you talk to your dad. Once we find the necklace, we'll need him on board. It's best to get a head start on this situation. It might take some coaxing to get him into the right headspace for what's to come.

I find myself in a moment of hesitation as my fingers hover over the keyboard, trying to think of my response when the little red battery icon appears, taunting me. A second later, my screen fades to black.

I take a deep breath, feeling a sense of relief wash over me. This problem can wait until tomorrow.

CHAPTER 28
WITCH GIRL

The sky above me is wicked and ready to open up, but I ignore the thunderous warning, as I'd rather be out here than inside.

Morning came too soon, and I'm not prepared to see my dad. I managed to miss him last night. So, now I'm sitting uncomfortably on the cool concrete steps outside of my house, trying to avoid him. I fear that when I see him, my eyes will betray the secrets I'm keeping.

I don't want my dad to be a part of this world—a world his mother purposefully kept him from. What good would it do to tell a middle-aged man that his entire life has been a lie? He's already faced enough if you ask me, including the hemlock poisoning and the nightmarish callings. Isobel said my dad couldn't be called, so what's the point of involving him? Look what happened to Mia. My dad is my rock and the only family I have left, and I can't risk losing him.

Could the extra necklace really belong to him anyway, when he's shown no signs of magic? As long as the final necklace remains out of our hands, my dad can stay blissfully unaware of his heritage. I'm not telling him until it's absolutely necessary. Plus, this should be my call, and no one else's. But does that make me selfish when everyone's magic is on the line and it's possibly our only chance to break the hunter's curse?

What if the necklaces are another trap—something the rival coven is using to lure us into the darkness and keep us broken forever?

Ugh!

I have yet to turn my phone back on from last night. Part of me thinks if I don't, then maybe yesterday didn't happen. Maybe Callen didn't really lie to me, and maybe I wasn't so gullible to believe everything he told me.

With my phone staring back at me, I decide to press the little button on the side and bring the thing back to life.

As I wait, the thick clouds above churn and contort with a dark, sinister energy. Their swirling mass gives me a glimpse of what's to come. A streak of lightning cracks through the sky like a whip. I count to three before the thunder booms in the morning sky. The storm's getting closer. Eventually, I'll have to go inside. My hopes of checking the fort today also seem to die with the weather. With my phone finally back on, I notice I have four messages waiting to be read.

Callen: Did you make it home? Being mad at me doesn't change the threats against you. Please text me.

Callen: You should be home by now. Please let me know.

Callen: Please respond. I'm getting worried, Izzy.

Callen: Since you didn't text me back, I drove by your house. Your bedroom light was on, so I'm going to assume you're safe. I'll always worry about you. I'll always try to protect you.

I take a deep breath and compose my response.

More like try to control me. I type the words, but delete them. He doesn't deserve my reply.

A bright bolt of lightning illuminates the dark sky above, putting on quite the show, while making my shadow dance along the sidewalk and taking my mind off Callen's text messages.

One, two—boom. It's getting closer.

Besides the flickering light show, something else catches my eye. I glance down the street. A young boy's watching me, while recklessly circling the street with his bike, not paying attention to the cars swerving around him. I cringe, parting my mouth, ready to tell him to watch out, but his cruel sneer causes me to pause.

"Hey, witchy, witch girl." His words catch me off guard, making me leap to my feet.

"What did you say?" I shout at the spiky-haired child.

It's just another voice in my ear. He didn't really say that, right?

"You heard me, witch girl."

I shake my head, dashing down the steps.

He's real, all right.

Standing on the curb, I holler again, "What did you say?"

"Why don't you use your witchy powers to rewind time, and then you'll know." He laughs.

"Little shit," I say under my breath. "Seriously, why did you say that?"

The boy hesitates, riding his bike in a figure eight before finally answering. "Your house is haunted, and the new mayor says there are witches in this town. The last lady that lived here was a witch, so you're a witch."

"He's not the mayor yet," I correct him. "Plus, here's an early lesson in life: you can't always believe everything a politician says. There are no witches in East Gate. So, can you go on now? Shoo," I gesture for him to keep riding, but he continues to taunt me.

"Witchy witch girl. You're a witch. You're gonna hang like the Salem witches."

"Seriously, go on. Get out of here, or I'm going to tell your parents."

His eyes glint with defiance and mischief. "You don't know who my parents are. Plus, they think you're a witch too."

The little shit is right. I have no idea who he is or where he lives.

"Witchy witch girl." A cruel smile fixes on his lips.

A sense of unease settles over me. This is bad. Really bad. I'm not afraid of this little kid, but Jessa's dad's campaign is built on a public safety platform full of fear and suspicion. He's stirring the pot, and now it seems like the townsfolk are along for the witch hunt.

This is the last thing my coven needs, especially with things being so delicate with my dad. This kid's probably not the only one ready to throw stones.

"Please go home," I say the words as the sky crackles, and a bright bolt of lightning tears through it, splitting the clouds wide open.

The sound of thunder roars through the air, shaking the ground beneath me, and rain pours down in sheets.

The young boy pedals away, his bike wheels splashing through the puddles already forming on the road. "Bye witchy witch girl," he shouts, nearly out of earshot, sticking his middle finger in the air as he disappears over the hill.

What the fuck?

I pivot to run up the steps as the storm intensifies. Another bolt of lightning illuminates the sky, followed closely by a deafening clap of thunder that echoes through the valley below. The rain grows heavier, soaking me through to the bone in a matter of seconds. I quickly make my way inside, my teeth chattering from the icy cold wetness that clings to my skin.

I'm surprised to see my dad when I enter the foyer, concern etched across his face.

"It's pouring out there," I say, responding to his curious gaze, as heavy raindrops pelt against the closed door.

"I can see that. What on earth were you doing out there?"

Avoiding you.

"I was, um, trying to get some fresh air. The house is so stuffy."

"Is it? I hadn't noticed," he responds. "You should go change into something dry and meet me in the dining room for breakfast. I picked up some pastries from East Gate Bakery before you were out of bed this morning. I think the trick is getting there early. For once, they had everything on the menu."

"Yummy. I can't wait to see what you got." I glide past

Dad, feeling the promise of my warm clothing upstairs calling to me.

"Hey, real quick," he says as my foot hits the first step. "I stopped by The Perk for a quick cup of joe, and Callen was working."

"Oh." My curiosity is piqued.

"He was acting strange, asking what you did last night."

"And?"

Dad clears his throat. "And—I told him I didn't see you come in last night. When I said that, his face turned white as a ghost. Is everything OK with you two?" Dad's brows knit together with concern.

"He's annoying me, that's all. It's fine," I reply, jolting upstairs.

Inside my room, I quickly take my phone out of my pocket. Using a towel, I wipe away the moisture before placing it on my desk. My home screen glows with a notification from Callen, but I choose to ignore it. He's a broken record.

I peel my wet clothes off and hang them on my chair to dry. I slide a green hoodie off the hanger and eagerly put it on, relishing in the softness of the fabric on my skin. I exchange my wet jeans for a pair of comfortable yoga pants and exit the room, leaving my buzzing phone behind me.

In the dining room, my eyes are drawn to an open box of pastries in the middle of the table. The alluring aroma of freshly baked goods fills the air, making my mouth water. They all look delicious.

"Dad, did you buy the place out?" I ask as Dad comes in with two plates.

"I couldn't decide, so I got one of everything," he chuckles. "At least we'll have breakfast sorted for a couple of days."

My gaze moves over the pastries, and I finally decide on a blueberry scone. I put it on my plate, but not before adding an old-fashioned doughnut alongside it. Dad goes for a flaky cheese danish and joins me at the table.

I sink my teeth into the freshly baked doughnut. The sweet taste fills me with satisfaction. This is exactly what I needed.

My dad's cheerful expression turns serious, and I place the doughnut back on the plate.

"It's quite gloomy inside the bakery nowadays. Not that I used to go in there a lot, but it's different," he says, his smile fading. "The atmosphere feels heavy with sadness. You know they've put up posters all over the walls about their missing employee."

I wouldn't know.

I haven't stepped foot in East Gate Bakery since the hunters killed Robin, the bakery lady. Guilt won't allow me back inside, even though they wanted to kill us first. It was us or them, but that still doesn't make things easy—another reason I can't let my dad into this world. He'd hate me if he knew I was involved in this mess.

"Oh, that's sad," I reply with a generic response for someone who knows the missing woman is dead.

I'm not feeling so hungry now. Memories of Bree gliding her knife along the bakery lady's throat, blood pouring out of her like a river and rushing toward me is enough to make me push my plate aside.

"East Gate's changing," my dad adds.

Good thing you didn't catch Joseph Dewitt's press conference yesterday.

"Anyway"—Dad smiles and takes a bite of his Danish— "I found something really cool in one of the bedrooms in the west wing, while I was clearing it out yesterday," he says excitedly while chewing.

Dad turns around and reaches for something wedged between the buffet table and the curio cabinet.

"Isn't this neat?" he exclaims, placing the item into my hands.

It's an old, dark wooden sign with the words 'Beswick Manor' etched into it.

"It's very beautiful," I respond.

He grins. "I think it's mahogany wood. It held up pretty good, don't you think? I don't recall ever seeing this hung, but it's perfect. I wanted to hang it outside on the front of the house today, but it looks like this storm isn't letting up anytime soon."

"Are you sure you want to hang it?"

"Of course. So many of the historic homes in this area have signs; ours should too."

Hanging this sign would be like waving a big red flag, reminding the town Beswicks still live here. Our name is forever associated with witches, and we don't need that attention right now.

"Maybe we should wait until we complete the repairs; it could be our finishing touch."

"Nah, it's going up soon."

Great.

CHAPTER 29
HUNTER SPEED

"How is it already Friday?" I say to the girl in the mirror, half expecting her to respond. I carefully pick up a vibrant purple hair extension and examine my reflection, trying to find the perfect spot to add the streak of color—my feeble attempt at showing some school spirit.

A glamour spell would be much easier.

"Rah Rah, go team," I mutter, carefully positioning the extension into the left side of my hair, making sure it fits perfectly.

School spirit isn't really my thing. I enjoy sports, but the whole idea of getting decked out is a little over the top. Nonetheless, I know Margo and Tahlia will be dressed in our school colors of purple and white, and I want to fit in. I reach for my East Gate High hoodie; the bold purple letters pop against the sleek white fabric, and I slide it over my T-shirt.

I'm as good as I'm going to get.

This entire week's been a straight-up blur between Callen's incessant text messages, none of which I've returned, to my many trips to the cottage. Scarlet hasn't come back, and maybe she was never even here to begin with. I'm starting to question my sanity again, and I don't like that one bit.

The good news is that we haven't had any more threats. Things almost seem at peace. Even Margo, Tahlia, and I are better—well, civil, but it's a start. Riley and I keep our distance, but it will be nice to watch him from afar tonight. Jessa—now that's a whole other beast of a problem. She must be so rattled by everything, but she hasn't said a word to us about any of it. I can't believe she's managed to avoid us this whole time. But bitchy girls will do bitchy things if it suits them, and Jessa is the master of doing whatever she pleases.

***

Stepping into the football stadium at the start of the second quarter, I'm struck by the sensation of the ground trembling beneath my feet, as the crowd stomps on the bleachers in sync with the iconic anthem, 'We Will Rock You' by Queen. It seems as if the entire town is here, which explains why so many businesses on my walk down Main Street had closed signs hung unusually early.

The scent of freshly popped popcorn and sizzling hotdogs wafts through the air as I pass by the concession stand that's run by the junior and senior DECA club, reminding me that my college applications are lacking in extracurricular activities. I've yet to receive an admission letter from the University of Connecticut. But I'm not thinking about that now; instead; I stride toward an open cashier, exchanging a five-dollar bill for a bag of popcorn beckoning from the window display.

With a handful of popcorn in my mouth, I set off to find my friends. The stands are a dizzying mix of purple and white, with cheering fans waving banners and flags.

It's only high school football, people.

But I guess they don't have the convenience of the Sea Hawks stadium just a stone's throw away, like I did when living in Seattle. This is their entertainment, and I shouldn't judge.

Among the crowd, I quickly spot Tahlia and Margo in the second row of bleachers. Tahlia looks stunning as always; her tight purple tank top contrasts beautifully with her white denim jacket. Both girls have their hair pulled into high ponytails with matching purple scrunchies. Margo's wearing a special football jersey with the name 'Calhoun' boldly printed on the back. The school's been selling them all week in Megan's memory, with all the proceeds benefiting her favorite charity. I guess they look nicer than the ones the football players made in her honor with tape and permanent marker. I wonder if Megan would understand the sentiment. It's not like she was a football player. She wasn't even a cheerleader, but who am I to say anything? It's partly my fault she's dead.

"How's the game?" I ask, dropping onto the cold bleacher seat next to Margo.

Tahlia slightly scoffs at me.

Margo offers me a kind smile, "Don't mind T; she's on edge today. But the game's going good so far. We're up by seven. Trevor Nolan scored two touchdowns in the first quarter and got a field goal." Her round eyes shine with pride. "Look at me, talking football. I'm actually just repeating what I heard someone else say," she admits. "Football or any sports aren't really my thing."

"You had me fooled." I laugh. "How's Riley doing?"

"I think good, but I really don't know. I haven't heard anyone say anything useful that I can repeat to make me sound smart." She fills the air around us with a light-hearted laugh that's infectious. "All I know is that he runs when the ball is tossed. So, that's got to count for something, right?" she says with a carefree shrug. Margo flashes a smile that lights up her face, then redirects her eyes back to the field.

I follow her gaze, and it leads me directly to Riley. He glides down the yard lines, his movements fluid and graceful, effortlessly evading the opposing team in blue. He catches the ball with a firm grip, and as he shifts his weight, his cleats dig into the ground, propelling him forward at an unbelievable speed that defies human capabilities.

Hunter speed.

The sight makes my skin crawl.

I quickly glance around, and the crowd roars, unaware of what they just witnessed, and thank goodness for that. He needs to be more careful.

"Hey, has anyone seen Jessa?" I scan the stadium, searching for Jessa's signature platinum blonde hair.

Before Margo can reply, a collective gasp escapes from the surrounding crowd. My eyes are drawn to the ungodly sight of Jessa walking in with Sam Hornsby.

I close my eyes momentarily, letting the image sink in and questioning its reality. But when I open my eyes, Jessa and Sam are still walking side by side, and it seems she's enjoying his company. Why is Jessa here with Sam Hornsby of all people? Especially after everything she knows. We framed him for a murder that she committed. She's playing with fire, and for what reason?

Tahlia leaps to her feet, her finger extended accusingly toward the pair. "What the hell is she doing with him?" Tahlia yelps, echoing my thoughts.

CHAPTER 30
STRANGE DUO

I lean into Margo, my eyes fixed on the strange duo. "Is she insane?"

Margo shakes her head in disbelief. "She's lost her mind."

The tension radiating from the people around us makes my blood boil, their hushed whispers filling my ears.

"Maybe we should have kept a closer eye on her," I suggest. My mind races as I try to make sense of what I'm seeing.

As the game continues, the couple becomes the center of attention, drawing the stares and whispered comments of those around us. "I can't believe that murdering psycho is here," one person says, their voice laced with disgust.

Another whispers, "How dare he show his face."

A third asks, "What is she doing with him?"

"Is Jessa trying to get her daddy's attention?" someone else chimes in.

"He will flip. He wants Sam behind bars," another person answers.

"He should be in jail," a final voice adds, their words punctuated by a sharp breath.

Their words have a sickening effect on my stomach, causing nausea to rise. We bear the guilt for Sam's unfortunate status as the school pariah.

"Bathroom, now," Tahlia demands.

The three of us rise and maneuver our way through the packed stands. I hum a little tune in my head to avoid overhearing any more chatter.

As we enter the bathroom, Tahlia takes the lead, passing by the sinks and gesturing for us to follow her into the stall at the end. I'm the last to enter. As I try to lock the door, I realize it doesn't work properly, so I lean against it.

"What are we going to do about Jessa?" Margo asks.

"Should we confront her?" I question.

Tahlia gives me an annoyed glare, her eyes narrowing in frustration.

Maybe it's not a good idea for two witches to be confined in a tight space with a possible transitioning hunter.

"I think it's time to pull off the Band-Aid and finally talk to her, but that's up to you, Margo," Tahlia responds.

Margo bites her bottom lip, while the irritatingly loud buzz of the fluorescent lights overhead adds tension to the silence between us.

With a loud bang, the entry door slams shut, making us all jump.

Tahlia softly utters, "Hush," while placing her finger against her mouth, signaling for silence.

The sound of heels clacking against the concrete floors echoes through the restroom, coming to a halt just outside the stall we're hiding in.

The door I'm leaning against swings open, sending me tumbling into Margo's arms.

Jessa storms in, her face twisting in anger. "Are you bitches going to avoid me forever?"

CHAPTER 31
GOOD RIDDANCE

The bathroom stall fills with a thick, suffocating tension that presses in on all sides as Jessa steps in and closes the door behind her.

I steady myself next to Margo.

"What the hell, Jessa?" Tahlia exclaims. Her mossy green eyes lock onto Jessa's piercing blue gaze, creating a tense standoff.

Jessa nonchalantly flips her hair over her shoulder, and a gentle waft of a floral fragrance fills the air. "Who I hang out with is none of your business," she snaps.

"But Sam?" I shift on my feet, trying to nestle myself behind Margo, who's standing quietly to my left, her arms crossed firmly under her chest, her anger percolating.

"It's not like I have anyone else to hang out with," Jessa replies.

Margo's face, once sprinkled with tiny and adorable freckles, now displays a unified and fiery crimson patch. Her body tenses next to mine.

"And whose fault is that, Jessa?" Margo steps forward, her voice dripping with disdain.

The lights above us crackle as if to punctuate Margo's question.

Jessa takes a step back, but hits the door. "Whatever. I see nothing's changed, so I'm going to go hang out with my other friend."

"You're playing with fire," I respond.

"No, that's you, Izzy. Oh, wait, that's right. Not anymore." Jessa pulls the door back, slipping through the tiny crack, leaving the three of us dumbfounded with our mouths hanging open.

"Should we go after her?" I ask.

"There's no point. Jessa's going to do what Jessa's going to do," Tahlia responds through clenched teeth, her eyes swirling with different shades of hate.

Margo pushes through Tahlia and I, exiting the stall first. "I want to go home."

"Me too," Tahlia responds. "Do you want a ride, Izzy? I have my dad's car."

"No, I'm going to walk."

"Suit yourself," Tahlia says.

***

Walking home, I'm overwhelmed by a concoction of emotions coursing through my body. I keep my head down as I pass the park. I don't need the reminder of what happened there last weekend to crawl into my brain. Callen—Riley— the pentagram. It's all too much.

I pick up my pace, the brisk wind kissing my cheeks, eager to get to my cozy bedroom and escape the world. All I want to do is put on my pj's and bury myself under my blankets. Is that too much to ask?

Apparently, it is.

As I approach Jefferson Place, I catch sight of the taunting kid from a few days ago, along with two taller boys, loitering on my steps. I cross the street, taking cautious footsteps, but they notice me. Their eyes lock onto mine, and a mischievous smirk forms on their lips, causing my heart to race.

"What the hell do you think you're doing?" I ask, slowly approaching them, trying to sound confident and brave.

"Just having a little fun, witch." One boy sneers, grinning wickedly. He's holding a can of spray paint.

I notice the letters W-I-T-C-H already outlined on the first step.

"This is private property!" I shout, trying to sound authoritative.

"Why don't you go back to the tunnels, witch?" the second taller boy says.

"What's with these frickin' tunnels?" The words roll off my tongue with annoyance.

"You're a witch, you should know," the little spiky-haired kid taunts.

"I'm calling the cops," I say, my voice shaking slightly. I pretend to dial and bring my phone to my ear.

"She's bluffing," the kid with the spray paint says confidently.

"Officer Tim Hawkins, it's Izzy," I say into a dead phone.

I cover the phone's speaker. "Officer Hawkins is a family friend," I snootily add.

The trio of juvenile delinquents search for truth in my words.

"I have three young boys here that are vandalizing my house. Can you come over?" I say into the phone. "They might be the ones that graffitied the gazebo."

What if they are the guilty ones? How would these twerps know about the chosen one, though?

"That's wonderful. You're about a block away. OK. See you soon," I respond into my phone.

Their gaze quickly shifts to panic. The spray paint drops from the taller boy's hand and rolls down to my foot. Frantically, they flee my property, darting through the neighbor's yard across the street and melting into the darkness of the night.

Good riddance.

I'm relieved, but also angry and a little heartbroken. It pains me to be the target of so much hate. Why do witches always get a bad rap? The bad seeds always ruin it for everyone.

Using the last remnants of the spray paint, I cover the words with a fresh layer and toss the can down the street. I don't mean to litter, but I don't have anywhere else to dispose of it without looking like the guilty party. I'll pick up every piece of litter I see for the next week to correct and restore my earthly karma.

I'm relieved when I finally push the front door open, but the sight of a newly hung sign to the right of the door makes me pause.

Dad hung the sign.
Beswick Manor.

CHAPTER 32
GIFTS

Stepping into my home, a chorus of unfamiliar laughter greets me. Its low bellowed pitch is hard to place, swirling around with my dad's joyous chuckle.

Who could be here?

"Izzy, is that you?" my dad calls out.

"Yes, I'm home from the game early." I walk through the maze of rooms, locating my dad in the dining room with Jonathan Kent.

"I didn't know you were coming over tonight," I say, directing my gaze to my new grandpa.

"Yup. Brought over some steaks and helped your dad with some things around the house," Jonathan responds.

"I noticed you hung the sign," I say.

"We sure did," Jonathan answers, sliding his plate back on the table and placing his hands on his stomach.

The mouthwatering scent of steak and roasted potatoes wafts through the air, making my stomach growl in hunger.

"Well, that was nice of you," I respond, making my way around the table and into the kitchen for a plate and cutlery.

Raising my voice, I shout through the rooms, "I didn't see your van outside."

"I took the old Chevy out tonight. The van's in the shop; it got vandalized," he responds, matching my pitch so I'll hear him.

Tell me something I don't know, Jonathan Kent.

With a frown properly etched on my face, I stroll back into the dining room. "Sorry to hear that."

"Mind if I have some?" I ask, already stabbing my fork into a hearty chunk of meat.

"Help yourself. We're just finishing up. It's all yours," Dad responds.

My eyes light up with delight as I heap potatoes onto my plate as well.

"Yeah, I noticed it when I left here that day. At first, I thought kids were just messing around in my van, but it turns out they vandalized it by smearing my own paint on the side." He pauses and shakes his head. "I can't be driving around like that, so I have a guy touching it up. Should be done in the morning."

Since they're bound to see it anyway, I might as well spill the beans that our steps were graffitied too. At least the word *witch* is gone.

"I think the same vandals spray painted our bottom step. I noticed some markings when I came home just now."

Dad tosses his hands in the air. "Oh, great. What's going on in East Gate? Jefferson Place is a beautiful street with historic homes. This shouldn't be happening. It kinda breaks my heart."

"I'm sure it's just a bunch of kids messing around. It will probably stop," I say, cutting my steak into bite-size pieces.

As I munch on my food, I silently observe my dad and new grandpa, the man I had suspected of threatening me. Seeing him here, sitting in dark blue denim and a button-up shirt, laughing with my dad, makes it all seem silly now. Callen was right. Jonathan Kent has nothing to do with any of this.

"So, are you going to the homecoming dance tomorrow night?" Dad asks, nearly making me choke on my food.

Oh, that's right, the homecoming dance.

I stir in my seat. "Um, I'm still not sure. I don't have a date, and I don't have a thing to wear."

"I hope you'll reconsider. It's your senior homecoming, sweetie. I think you'd regret it if you miss it."

"You know, your grandma and I went to homecoming together." The corners of Jonathan's mouth tug upward. "I can still picture Anna's beautiful pink dress swaying as we danced the night away. It was truly a magical evening."

Maybe more magical than you thought.

"Aww, that's so sweet. It sounds like you really loved her." I smile.

"I did. She was the love of my life. You know first loves are the hardest to lose." He drops his head.

My heart is flooded with a rush of anguish as I think of Riley, but just as quickly as Riley enters my thoughts, Callen appears. I've experienced the pain of losing two loves. My heart is so broken it may never mend.

My dad clears his throat as if clearing the air, creating a shift.

"I'm so glad our paths crossed finally." A few tears collect on his bottom eyelashes. "After my wife died, then my gran, and recently, my mom, I thought it would only be me and Izzy. After so much loss, it's nice to have gained something."

Jonathan's face glows, and his cheeks turn a jolly red. "I understand exactly what you mean."

I yawn, stretching my arms dramatically over my head. "I think I'm going to sneak off to bed and let you two continue your night."

Dad's brows raise. "Are you sure, sweetheart? You're more than welcome to stay and hang out."

"I know, Dad, but I'm tired." I pat my mouth, producing a fake yawn that turns into a real one.

"Oh, before I forget. A package arrived for you. It's on your bed."

"A package?" I question. "From whom?"

"I'm not sure. It was on the doorstep when Jonathan showed up."

"It's a nice-looking package," Jonathan adds.

"Well, now you've both got me curious, so I'm going to head upstairs. Goodnight."

"Goodnight," they both respond.

***

Resting gently on top of the bed is a stunning, oversized ivory box, adorned with a luxurious black silk bow. I delicately untie it, feeling the smoothness of the silk against my fingertips.

I gently raise the lid of the box, unveiling a mysterious object swathed in dark, velvety tissue paper, with a small card atop it. I carefully pull out the note from inside the envelope, revealing the message: *Wear Me Tomorrow.*

With excitement, I unwrap the tissue paper and gently pull the item from the box. It's a beautiful black dress with a tulle skirt and sheer overlay.

I quickly undress and slip the garment over my body, then I walk over to my mirror to examine it closely. The fluffed-out skirt falls just above my knees, creating a stunning silhouette that adds a touch of whimsy, making it truly stunning. The dress hugs my body in all the right places. I love it.

But who is it from—Riley, Callen, or one of the girls? The note failed to reveal the mysterious sender of this magical dress. The sheer elegance of the box makes me think it's Callen. But it's not like I can ask him, because if it's not from him, he will assume it's from Riley and vice versa. That's a pot I can't stir tonight.

I gently take off the gorgeous dress and hang it in my wardrobe. I change into my cozy clothes and lift the box off my bed, only to find another little gift beneath it. Dad didn't say anything about two packages. This one is much smaller and wrapped in brown craft paper. It's not nearly as elegant as the first package.

I tear into the paper, and it's not a gift I see; it's Callen's Book of Shadows.

CHAPTER 33
MY BELOVED IZZY

The stunning green leather-bound book invites me to open it. However, the memory of being reprimanded for looking at it without permission lingers, and it feels like an invasion of privacy to do so again. Nevertheless, I can't ignore the fact that the book is here for a reason. With trembling hands and a deep breath, I gather the courage to flip the cover open. Inside, a note on elegant stationery embellished with a delicate floral design awaits me.

My Beloved Izzy,

I want to start by apologizing for the pain I've caused you. It wasn't my intention to betray your trust, but I do understand why you feel that way.

To show you I'm committed to being open and honest with you from now on, I would like you to read my Book of Shadows. It will give you a better understanding of where I'm coming from, and I hope you'll see that my intentions are good. If, after reading my book of shadows, you feel that you can forgive me and trust me again, I would be honored if you would join me at the dance tomorrow night.

Yours forever and always, Callen

The world spins out from under me, leaving me twisted with anticipation and confusion. In my hand, I hold Callen's Book of Shadows with his permission to continue. His personal grimoire that contains everything he's documented since becoming a witch. My heart races with excitement and an eagerness to see what lies beyond these pages.

I take his note, tracing my fingers over his handwriting before pulling it close to my heart. "Don't disappoint me, Callen," I say out loud, as if he can hear me.

As I turn the pages gilded in gold, some passages leap off the page, as if the calligraphy is infused with a magical energy, drawing me to it.

There's a shift in the air. Something extraordinary is about to happen. I can't quite put my finger on it, but the atmosphere is in a state of flux, like something is shifting beneath the surface of the earth, aligning itself in perfect harmony. Someone is coming. Could it be another witch? Whoever it is, she's important.

He already admitted to sensing me before we met, but failed to mention the powerful feelings it stirred inside of him. I can't believe I had that kind of impact on someone. The intensity of his initial connection to me fills me with flashes of warmth that spread through my body from the inside out, reminding me of my lost fire. I wrap my arms around my chest, holding tightly to prolong the sensation, but it passes, and I turn the page to view the next passage.

Today, I finally saw her—the one I've been waiting for all summer. I was beginning to think she wasn't coming. But then she walked into the coffee shop as if the timing was always meant to be this way. The air electrified around her, coming to life as she moved through the shop. Her presence was magnetic, and I was drawn to her like a moth to a flame.

My attraction to her almost frightened me at first because I'd never felt anything so intense before. I could sense what she needed, which worked perfectly to my advantage. When I passed her an iced mocha with extra everything, our fingers grazed, and I could see her thoughts and so much more. She needs my help, and I'll do everything in my power to protect her because she's special.

She's a Beswick. She's like me.

Seeing his words displayed so vulnerably on the page makes my heart yearn for Callen, but his betrayal still lingers in the air like a burnt-out candle. I move on without pausing to read the next page, which contains the connection spell. I don't need to read that one again.

I have a connection with Izzy that doesn't require a spell. Our touch sends shock waves through my body, and I can't risk changing a thing in fear of losing this special power. We've been gifted the power of touch and sight. I can keep her safe. We're kindred spirits. I did what I had to do to keep her and the girls safe. We're a strong coven of four now, pulling from the earth's gifts. I'll help Izzy perfect her powers, and together we'll make things right. Even though my heart knows the truth, Izzy's heart still longs for a hunter. I can only be her friend for now, but I know we'll find our way to each other.

My heart lurches as I continue to the next passage.

Izzy's drawn to the hunter. His eyes are shifting, and he's changing fast. His tattoo is near completion. It's only a matter of time. I need to keep her safe. I fear Tahlia will follow next. There must be something we can do. We must find a way to break the hunter's curse once and for all, even if that means I lose my soulmate by setting the hunter free.
At least I'll know she's happy.

Tears race down my cheeks. Everything Callen's done is for the good of our coven. There isn't a selfish bone in his body; I see that now. His notation of Riley and Tahlia and the hunter's curse makes my skin prickle—we've failed them. We're no closer to setting them free from the spell that bounds them to a life of hunting witches.

I browse the rest of the entries, mostly spells that are no longer useful without our magic. In fact, he hasn't created a new entry since he lost his magic, expect for one—another note for me.

Izzy,
If you're still reading this, I want to say that despite our lost magic, we still have strong feelings for each other. Magic was never necessary for us to be together. I may not be able to hear your thoughts or share

your visions, but our bond as kindred spirits is unbreakable. I hope that will count for something. Friends or lovers, I'll take whatever you can give me.

Forever and always, Callen

CHAPTER 34
GAME OF TELEPHONE

"Izzy, it's almost seven. You're going to be late," my dad's words carry down the hallway and into my bedroom.

I quickly glance at the clock on my phone; he's right. I lost track of time while fussing with my hair. I want it to be as perfect as the dress I'm wearing. I have a feeling tonight is going to be magical, and I want everything perfect.

It needs something still, though.

I reach for Gran-gran's black and silver barrette, delicately placed in a dish on my vanity table and carefully secure it in my hair, taming my wild, full, round-barrel curls and adding a touch of elegance to complement my beautiful dress.

"I'm coming!" I shout, flying down the hallway.

As I descend the old wooden staircase of our Italianate-style home, feeling like a princess in a fairy tale, my dad freezes in his tracks.

"Wow, sweetheart, you look incredibly beautiful." A grin spreads across his face, accompanied by the glimmer of a tear in the corner of his eye. "I wish your mother could see what a beautiful and smart young woman you've turned into."

Or disappointed by the secret keeping witch I've become.

"Thank you, Dad."

"Was that dress in the nice package that was left for you yesterday?" Dad asks, eyeing my exceptionally spectacular dress.

"Yes, it's from Callen."

"So, the two of you are good?"

"Yes." I proudly smile, feeling like for once, something is going right.

My dad's gaze drops to my feet. "Converse sneakers? You don't have anything nicer?" he asks, a bit disappointed.

"I had nothing that would work, and Callen didn't include footwear in the box," I sheepishly respond, awkwardly crossing my legs as if it could hide my shoes.

Dad frowns. "Izzy, I'm sure you have something better than sneakers."

"At least they're all black," I mutter, taking the final steps, meeting my dad in the foyer.

He slips his coat on. "Whatever. You're going to be late, so we better get going."

I pass by the hall tree mirror, catching a glimpse of a flickering flame dancing behind my passing reflection.

Not today.

***

From a distance, I spot Callen waiting for me on the school's front steps, looking dapper in a sleek black suit and stylish purple bow tie.

"Have fun, sweetie," Dad says.

"Thanks, Dad," I respond, my fingers already wrapped around the door handle, ready to leap out of the car.

Callen greets me with a warm smile, his eyes twinkling with hope as I approach him. The last thing he wrote in his book flickers across my mind like a neon sign—*Friends or lovers, I'll take whatever you can give me.*

"You came," he says with delight. "I take it you got my gift. I hope it's OK that I'm here."

"I'm so sorry," I say, my voice breaking as I toss my arms around his neck, pulling him close.

"I missed you, Beswick," Callen whispers into my ear.

His divine scent stirs around his subtle movement, making me go weak in the knees. All I can think about is kissing him, but right now isn't the place.

"Should we talk about it?" Callen asks, pulling away from me, leaving a small part in the space between us.

A stray curl of Callen's hair defies his tightly wound tendrils, playfully draping itself over his forehead. I reach my hand up and gently tuck it back into place. My eyes are drawn into his as we stand in silence, our gazes locked intently on one another.

I shake my head. "Not here," I respond. "How about we don't think about anything tonight? Let's just see what happens. Maybe we try to create a re-do of our relaxing evening that got ruined? I think we owe it to ourselves to unwind and have some fun."

"That sounds perfect." He gleams.

"Hey, where are the girls?" I ask, my gaze floating from one side of the building to the other, expecting them to be close by.

"Margo wanted to talk to Megan."

My eyebrow rises involuntarily.

"The pond," he responds.

"Oh, their special place. That makes sense."

"Yeah, my dad drove her there, then he's dropping her off here. She should arrive soon. They left before me."

"And Tahlia?"

"She's still getting ready. Tahlia's never on time for these things. My mom's dropping her off."

Shivering from the cold, I rub my bare arms to warm myself. "Should we go inside?" I ask, peering through the cracked double door.

His hand clasps mine tightly, and together we step into the school.

"I'm a little disappointed. I thought it'd be more decorated," I say.

Callen laughs. "The dance is in the south gym, not the hallway, weirdo."

"The dances at my previous school were always held in big venues. So, I didn't know what to expect. I thought there'd be some grand entrance."

He pinches the skin between his eyes and shakes his head. "Oh, Beswick, you're something else."

"Hey, now," I respond, readying myself to playfully slug him in the shoulder.

But before I can move, he grabs my wrists and twirls me around, surprising me.

"You look absolutely stunning, by the way," he says.

"Thank you," I respond, my smile radiating and confidence soaring. "How did you know my size?" I ask, twirling around a second time, relishing in the sensation of the tulle skirt floating around me.

He furrows his brow, looking puzzled.

My heart plummets like a heavy weight, sinking into the depths of my chest. "The dress isn't from you?"

"No, I'm sorry. It's not from me, but you look amazing in it."

I stop, stunned in place. "It was on my bed with your book. Didn't you leave both packages on the doorstep?"

"No, just the one, and I didn't leave it on your doorstep. I couldn't chance my book being seen by anyone but you. I covertly slipped into your house when your dad came home from work and left it on your bed for you to find after the game. There were no other packages when I was there."

"Then who sent me this beautiful dress?"

"Riley." A low, menacing hiss escapes Callen's lips.

In an instant, the serene hallway transforms into a bustling scene, alive with the sounds of chatter and laughter, as students skirt around us, adding to the disruption of my almost perfect moment.

Standing in front of my date, wearing a dress meant for another boy, makes me sick to my stomach.

How could I have been so wrong?

I was certain this dress was from Callen. The guilt I know so intimately well crawls through my body like a disease, invading every organ.

"I need to use the restroom." I shove past Callen and race down the B wing to the nearest bathroom.

"I'll meet you inside the gym," Callen hollers, his voice fading with my increased speed.

Inside the bathroom, I want to splash water over my face, but I don't want to ruin my perfect hair and makeup. Instead, I stomp my feet hard into the ground like a little child throwing a tantrum.

What did I think was going to happen tonight? That I'd have some magical evening with Callen and completely avoid Riley? The air grows dense around me, nearly suffocating me.

How could I be so stupid?

I was so wrapped up in the excitement of the dress and Callen's book that I let myself forget one simple fact—I still have two boys that I love. One, a hunter in, 'Let's not attack Izzy the witch' training, and the other, a witch who already loves me with all of his heart. I have to get my heart straight and figure out what I truly want, although I think I already know the answer.

I'm going to break someone's heart tonight.

Pull your shit together, Izzy. You can't hide in this bathroom forever.

A bathroom stall swings open, and a nameless but familiar junior girl emerges, making her way over to the sink and washing her hands next to me.

Shit, I thought I was alone.

She reaches into her purse and retrieves a tube of red lipstick, passing it to me with a smile. "You need a pop of color."

Without hesitation, I grab the lipstick and glide it across

my lips, staining them a bold, cherry red.

"Much better." The girl smiles at our reflections while adjusting her hair in the mirror.

"Thanks," I mutter, popping my lips.

She flips her silky red hair over her shoulder. "Do you think Jessa will show up with Sam tonight?"

I scrunch my nose. "I'm not sure. We're not on the best of terms right now."

"I don't think I'd be talking to her either. She's a bitch, and she only does what serves her. She's always been like that. Although my friends and I can't figure out what serves her with Sam Hornsby." She puckers her lips and reapplies her lipstick with the same shade she passed me. "He's not even hot. I mean, I get it if he was a hottie like Riley Hawkins or Trevor Nolan. Those boys could get away with murder and still be popular, but Sam's a C-list boy and guilty of murder."

"He's not guilty, though," I say under my breath. "And he's not that bad looking." *In a certain light.*

"He's a dog. I guess we'll never find out if he's truly guilty, since he won't have his day in court. So, as far as most of the town's concerned, he's guilty."

I frown at my reflection in the mirror.

"See you inside the dance," the girl says, waving her hand in the air before vanishing behind the door.

What a bitch.

I'm tempted to wipe away the lipstick in spite. But as I bring my hand to my mouth, I stop. She's right; I did need that pop of color. It's too pretty to waste. *Dang it.*

***

I feel so far away, yet the dance is merely down the hall. I shouldn't be here. Thoughts of turning around and exiting the school call to me from every direction, but I dismiss them and follow the pulsating vibrations emanating from the homecoming dance.

The south gymnasium's been magically transformed into a sparkling space of elegance with glittering streamers, balloons, and twinkling lights. The only evidence that it's a gym is the basketball hoops suspended from the ceiling, but even those are covered in streamers and lights.

I scan the crowd, spotting a few familiar faces, but I can't find Callen, Riley, or the girls. A group of students huddled together gossiping grabs my attention. A blonde girl whispers to her friend, who passes it on to another girl, creating a chain of secrets like a game of telephone. The whispers spread until the entire gym is filled with a low hum of chatter.

Unable to resist my curiosity, I follow the pointed fingers and accusing eyes to find out what's causing all the excitement.

They're pointing at me.

CHAPTER 35
A WITCHY STATEMENT

The crowd slowly parts, opening a straight path for my hero. Callen takes confident strides toward me, his handsome figure illuminated by the twinkling lights. As he approaches me, a flicker of unease flashes in his velvety eyes. He pulls me close, his warm breath grazing my neck.

Instead of kissing me like heroes often do, he whispers, "Just smile and don't say anything."

I obey, flashing a forced grin. He gently hooks his arm through mine and leads me along the edge of the gym until we find a hidden nook concealed behind the refreshment table that's draped with a shimmery black tablecloth. A row of faux crystal bowls sits atop the table, filled to the brim with crimson punch, creating a barrier between us and the curious gazes of the student body.

"Now, are you going to tell me why everyone is staring at me?" I demand.

"Riley didn't send you that dress," Callen replies.

Riley materializes from the shadows of the dance hall, keeping a safe distance.

"Riley?" I sputter in shock.

"Izzy, that dress isn't from me," Riley responds.

"OK, so it's not from either of you, but that still doesn't answer why everyone's staring at me." I spin around. "Is there something on me? Is the dress ripped?"

"No, it's not that, Izzy," Callen explains.

"Look." Riley points.

I struggle to catch my breath, my jaw dropping wide open as Tahlia and Margo approach from opposite directions of the gym.

"They're wearing my dress!" I cry out.

"I guess I didn't get the memo," Jessa's voice sneaks up from the end of the refreshment table, her tone laced with a hint of amusement. "That's why everyone's staring, Izzy."

Tahlia's confidently strutting across the dance floor, wearing my dress but accessorized better with strappy black high heels and a red sheer crop cardigan. Everyone's eyes are on her, and the same hushed whispers echo through the air. However, she doesn't seem to be fazed by it like I was.

"The sight of the three of you wearing the exact same dress is hilarious," Jessa adds. "I can't help but wonder why you're doing it. Are you trying to make some sort of witchy statement? I don't think that's very smart."

I let out a frustrated huff. "Trust me, it's not intentional." I scowl. "We're not exactly parading our witchiness around, especially since your dad's fueling a witch hunt. We aren't adding fire to that fuse."

Tahlia glides behind the table, positioning herself right next to Riley. "What the hell?" she mouths silently, her eyes narrowing in frustration.

I hunch my shoulder up in a shrug.

Confusion crosses Margo's face as she joins our ever-growing huddle of misfits. The only difference between our outfits is her black flats.

"Was this you?" Margo eyes Jessa.

Jessa fills up a cup of punch and takes a sip. "No, but it's funny."

Is it wrong to hope she spills her punch down the front of her tight white dress? Where's the magic when I really need it?

"All right, you guys are boring me. I'm going to go find my date. Tootles." She casually waves us off and disappears into the lively crowd of dancing students.

"OK, seriously. What the hell is going on?" I ask.

Tahlia's fingers instinctively reach up to tug at the unruly curl brushing against her cheek. "I had a gorgeous dress picked out. I even had it on, but then this dress showed up addressed to me. I thought it was too breathtaking not to wear."

"Did you question who it was from?" I ask.

"Nah. My parents are always spoiling me with nice clothes, so I assumed it was one of their surprises."

Must be nice.

"I don't think this was your parents, Tahlia. And your mom didn't mention it when she saw you in the dress?"

"No," Tahlia replies. "How did you get it?" She nods at me.

"My dad said it was in a box on the front steps. Someone delivered it," I inform them. "Margo, where did you find your dress?"

"When I came back from my morning walk, I found it

waiting on the doorstep. It was addressed to me with a note that said, 'Wear me tonight.' The allure of the beautiful dress was too strong to resist, especially considering I would have ended up wearing the same dress I wore last year. I assumed it was Jessa trying to apologize with her usual Jessa flair."

I furrow my brows, giving her a puzzled look.

"Her only love language is gifts," she answers.

"Oh," I respond. "So, if none of us sent them, why did someone go through the trouble, and what's their motive?"

"Check your doorbell cameras," Riley suggests, his voice tense.

"My house doesn't have a doorbell, let alone a camera," I respond, taking a slow step away from Riley, fearing I may be too close for him to handle.

Callen's tapping away on his phone, his expression growing more confused by the second. "There's nothing from the last twenty-four hours."

"Who cares?" Tahlia mutters under her breath, not bothering to hide her apathy or the hunter side that's seeping out. "Someone clearly played a dumb prank on us, but joke's on them. I'm not letting this dress go to waste, and neither should you two. I'm going to dance." Tahlia pulls Riley by the tie toward the dance floor, and Riley doesn't resist.

"But——" I call out.

Neither of them turns back.

"I'm going to join them. It's been a fucked-up year so far. I look good, and I want to enjoy the night," Margo says, chasing after Tahlia and Riley.

"Callen, don't you think this is odd?" I ask.

"Very," he responds, his brow raised. "Something's not adding up. I highly doubt someone here sent those dresses as a prank. There's no motive."

"Right," I agree.

"But the girls are right. We're already here, so maybe we could try to enjoy the night. Remember, it's a re-do of our relaxing evening." He nudges me. "No one's been harmed by this stupid prank."

I produce a half-grin. "I find that hard to do given the circumstances, but I suppose I can try."

With a warm smile, he extends his hand, his eyes sparkling. "Come on," he says, his voice filled with charm. "At least do me the honor of one dance."

The gentle touch of our hands ignites a rush of warmth, causing heat to creep across my face.

"This might set Riley off, and I don't want to deal with that tonight," I respond.

"He doesn't have to see us," Callen murmurs, guiding me to the far end of the dance floor, away from Riley's line of sight, yet right in Jessa's view.

"Fine," I reluctantly agree. "I guess one dance can't hurt."

He gently tugs my arm toward him, securing me tightly against his chest. His other hand gracefully wraps around my waist, settling delicately on the small of my back. He sways to a rhythm that doesn't quite align with the music blasting through the speakers.

"Callen, it's not a slow song," I point out.

"It doesn't matter to me, Beswick."

I can't help but give in to the moment and rest my head on his shoulder. Everything seems perfect until our third spin around when I notice something strange. Jessa keeps nervously glancing at her phone; her expression is filled with panic. I keep a close eye on her, observing the quick, darting movements of her eyes as they scan the room. Something has her on edge.

"Jessa's acting unusual," I whisper into Callen's ear, trying to keep my voice low.

"So, what?"

"So, I'm worried. Every few seconds, she pulls out her phone, and each time, her face goes white."

I maneuver us around, so Callen can get a better look. "See, she's doing it again.

"I wouldn't worry about it. She hasn't worried about any of us this past month."

"Fine," I respond, still keeping my eyes on Jessa.

Callen swings me around, picking up the pace to match the tempo of the next song. As he spins me around, waves of laughter escape my lips, but on the last twirl, I catch a fleeting sight of Jessa's blonde hair rushing toward the exit. Before I can even speak, Tahlia's at our side, her expression grave.

"Jessa's in trouble. We have to go."

CHAPTER 36
I KNOW WHAT YOU DID

We're racing down the hallway, the walls blurring past us as we sprint after Tahlia.

Dang, that girl can run in heels like nobody's business.

"Where are Margo and Riley?" I ask, panting, my breath coming in short, rapid bursts.

"They're ahead of us," she responds, her words spiked with frustration, failing to even turn her head in the slightest.

As we round the corner of the C wing, keeping our steady pace, Tahlia's ruby red cardigan slips off her shoulder.

"Tahlia, your arm!" Callen shouts.

The three of us come to an abrupt stop, our eyes locking on Tahlia's exposed arm. I gasp, but quickly cover my mouth.

The delicate beginnings of a design are taking shape on Tahlia's toned bicep—a hunter's tattoo.

We're too late. It's happening.

"Tahlia?" Fear lodges deep in my throat, making it hard to breathe.

She yanks her cardigan up. "Don't worry about it. I'm fine."

"But, Tahlia," Callen presses.

"No, I'm not talking about it." Tahlia resumes her quick pace down the hallway, her heels clicking on the polished floor. "Can you two slow pokes pick up the pace?"

"Where are we going?" I ask.

She stops again, her curly hair bouncing wildly on top of her head as she twists around. A swirling red glint envelops her eyes, slowly fading her green into the background. "The library," she responds, her lip curling upward in revulsion as if the sight of us is making her not only angry but sick to her stomach.

Callen's hand clasps mine tightly as we follow behind her at a much safer distance than before. He's trying to be brave, but his hand is trembling inside of mine.

The library appears empty when we arrive, but we follow Tahlia inside, anyway. As we walk past the rows of shadowy bookshelves, my eyes struggle to adjust to the dimness.

"Can we turn on a light?" I suggest, but no one responds.

"Hello," Tahlia calls out into the darkness.

"Over here." Riley's voice echoes through the silent library, beckoning us to the center, where we find him and Margo seated comfortably on the green, scratchy couches, each occupying their own space. A sizable area rug lies between them, creating separate territories—one side for the hunter and one for the witch.

Riley's eyes meet mine, and they flicker to my hand clasped with Callen's. I instinctively drop his hand. Thankfully, Callen doesn't react.

"Where the hell is Jessa?" Tahlia demands; her voice is sharp and assertive.

"She's not in here. I think she's messing with us, T," Margo responds.

"It's not T; it's Tahlia!" She stomps her stylish heel into the tan carpet, and collectively the witches in the room inch backward. "I don't want to be called T anymore. Got it?"

Riley walks across the geometric patterned rug, meeting Tahlia on the other side. He gently rests his hand on her shoulder. Calming breaths escape her lips, synchronizing perfectly with the moment her eyes regain their vibrant green hue.

Riley, the hunter whisperer. Too bad he can't calm himself down like that.

Tahlia shakes her arms out at her sides and flashes Riley a somber smile. He touches her shoulder once again, and Tahlia seems back to normal.

Just how close are the two of you getting?

I shake the idea from my head.

Tahlia skirts behind us, poking her head down each row of books. "Jessa!" she calls out.

"I'm so confused." I drop down next to Margo.

"Tahlia got a text from Jessa telling her she's in trouble and to meet her here, but I think it's part of an elaborate prank, and so are these dresses." She pats down the tulle skirt that keeps fluffing up at her. "I'm over her childish games, but Tahlia thinks she's in real trouble."

"Margo, she seemed scared at the dance. I saw her checking her phone multiple times before she ran out of the room," I respond.

"Where the hell is she?" Tahlia shrieks.

A ping, a buzz, and a vibration emanate from my phone, along with Tahlia's and Margo's, halting everyone's actions as if on cue to her question.

"What's going on?" Callen glances over my shoulder from behind the couch. "Is that a screenshot?"

Callen's right. It's a screenshot from Jessa. Everyone falls silent as we read her message.

Unknown number: I know what you did.
Unknown number: Your secrets can't stay buried forever; neither can your Jeep.

I gulp. *The Jeep.*

Callen squeezes my shoulder, and my eyes well with tears. I let out a deep sigh, and my eyes fall back to the screenshot, my stomach twisting into a pretzel.

Unknown number: I wouldn't ignore me.
Jessa: Who the hell is this?
Unknown number: You'll find out soon . . .

An ear piercing, shrill, high-pitched scream tears through the air, shattering the silence around us.

"Jessa!" Tahlia shouts, kicking off her high heels. She zooms past us before I can even send the message to my legs to stand.

The shrill scream infiltrates the air again, sending a tidal wave of fear through my body, rocking me upright.

CHAPTER 37
SATAN'S TUNNEL

Riley shoots past us, his body a blur—that whole hunter speed thing coming in handy.

The three witches—Margo, Callen and I—hurriedly follow behind. Margo takes the lead, her head twisting back to us as she continues forward.

"I can never forgive her, but—" her voice trails off.

"I know, Margo," I respond, coming up behind her.

As we sprint through the library, the rows of shelves become a mere blur in my peripheral vision, but amid our frenzied rush, a sudden flash of something attracts my attention. With no delay, I come to a stop and firmly pull Callen back. Without a word, I point, beckoning him to take a closer look.

"Keep going, Margo," I shout.

Callen's eyes shift forward, fixating on the far end of the last bookshelf. "Another pentagram." With a swift motion, he reaches for his phone and takes a snapshot. "That's the third one."

"Fourth," I sheepishly respond. "I actually found another

one the day I walked home from your house. It's Scarlet," I respond.

"Everything's connected," he says, yanking me out of the library.

The dripping red words in the bottom of the pentagram, *TONIGHT IT ENDS*, haunt me as we race through the school.

The loud pulsating beats echo down the hallway, blocking out any evidence something tragic is happening.

"Outside," Callen hollers, pulling me behind him.

We race down the steps and out the front door, finding our friends hurled over in defeat.

"She's gone." Tahlia sniffles.

"Shit!" Callen responds.

"Maybe Sam knows what happened," I suggest.

Riley yanks his phone out of a pocket inside his suit jacket. "I'll text him."

Almost immediately, his phone dings. "He hasn't seen her since they arrived at the dance."

"Great!" Tahlia shouts.

Margo's eyes light up. "Tahlia, remember that time Jessa made us turn on our location, so she could track us last summer? I turned mine off, but Jessa probably forgot all about it."

"Brilliant, Margo." Tahlia stares at her phone. "Yes! She's still sharing her location with me."

"Where is she?" Margo asks.

"Right now, it looks like she's by Izzy's house." She scrunches up her face. "No, she's still moving. She's going further away from town, toward the edge of the forest off Highway 31, in the lowlands."

"Where the hell is she going?" I ask.

"Her phone stopped moving." Tahlia flashes the screen to Riley. "Where could she be going all the way out there?"

"I think I know where she's heading." Riley gulps. "Satan's Tunnel."

CHAPTER 38
URBAN LEGENDS

"Will someone please fill me in? What's Satan's Tunnel?" I demand.

"We'll explain, but we need to get out of here. Who has a car?" Margo asks.

Callen and Riley raise their hands.

"I need better shoes." Tahlia's bare toes curl in the whispering wind. "My gym locker," she mutters.

"Go." Riley nods to her.

With a burst of energy, Tahlia sprints through the double doors.

"I'll wait for Tahlia. You three should go. We'll be right behind you. Be safe." Riley's eyes lock onto mine, and his piercing blue shines through.

He's still in there somewhere.

"Should we text our dads?" Riley asks.

"No, they'll try to stop us. I think this is something we have to do without them," Callen responds.

We cross the parking lot, locating Callen's Cadillac in the far-right corner of the lot.

"Seatbelts," Callen says, swiftly reversing and pulling the car onto the street. He accelerates as if speed limits don't exist.

"So, Satan's tunnel. What is it?" I press.

A heavy sigh escapes Callen's lips. "It's a network of tunnel systems that used to be the town's only water supply back when East Gate was founded. They've been out of commission for nearly a hundred years. But there's an urban legend that surrounds it. It's said that if you enter the tunnel at night, the devil will greet you with an offer."

"Great, it's nighttime," I huff. "What's the offer?"

"A sacrifice in exchange for anything you desire. If you accept the offer, you belong to him. If you deny him, you're cursed. Rumors are that brave souls who fail to heed the warnings come back hearing strange noises, seeing mysterious shadows, and with the unshakable feeling of being watched—if they return at all. But these are just stories. Kids love to come out here and mess around."

"But that's not the only urban legend," Margo adds. "There's another rumor about witches using the tunnels as a secret meeting place to perform their dark ritual practice of bringing people back from the dead."

"Necromancy," I say under my breath.

"But these are all just rumors," Margo says.

"Yeah, so was Isobel being a witch, and that turned out to be very, very true," I respond.

"We're here." Callen turns off his headlights and slowly comes to a park on a dark street with no other cars.

"There's no one here," I say.

"Her phone says she's here," Callen responds.

"Should we wait for Tahlia and Riley?" Margo asks with a layer of fear coating her voice.

"Jessa's in trouble. We can't wait, but let's hope for all our sakes that this is some stupid joke, and she's OK." Callen nods for us to exit the car.

I half expect Jessa and Sam to jump out at us and tell us they pulled the best prank on us, and we should see our faces, but nothing of that sort happens.

Margo steps out into the darkness first.

I twist to exit the car, but Callen stops me, pulling on my arm until I'm facing him. "Beswick, I don't know what's going to happen tonight—"

He leans in. As his lips touch mine, a wave of tingling sensations courses through my body, fueling my desire to kiss him back even more.

"Oh, Callen," I say between parted lips.

"We can talk later," he responds, pulling away, ending our kiss. "Margo's waiting outside."

My breath catches in my throat, and my lips quiver, desperately wanting to greet his sweet kiss again, but it doesn't happen. Instead, we both step out of the car and gaze at the dark forest ahead. The tall trees loom over us, and a cold breeze sweeps past us, sending shivers down my spine. Goosebumps rise on my skin as I take in the eerie silence of the forest.

"Do you feel that?" I ask, my voice shaking slightly.

"Feel what?" Margo questions.

"A pull to the forest," I respond.

They both nod, linking our arms, creating a sense of

unity amidst the eerie quietness. We begin our journey into the forest.

"I think it's only a quarter mile in. We should be there in no time," Callen whispers as if the trees have ears.

In the soft glow of the nearly full moon, a network of abandoned tunnels becomes visible. Callen quietly peeks into the first tunnel. The faint sound of trickling water echoes within its depths.

"There's no one here," he says softly.

As we walk through the mushy field of mossy green grass, the scent of damp earth fills the air.

The closer we get to the second tunnel, the more we notice a soft glow seeping out, illuminating the surrounding darkness.

"Shhh," Callen instructs, lifting his pointer finger in front of his mouth. "Someone's in there."

The sound of approaching footsteps startles me. My heart sinks. I turn around quickly, but I'm relieved to see the faces of Riley and Tahlia.

We're all together now.

"I'll go first," Callen says.

"No, we're all going together," I respond.

We quietly approach from the side, coming up on a tunnel made of old bricks that have been eroded by the passage of water and time.

"This one's longer than the first," Callen says in a hushed voice.

The five of us stare down the creepy entryway, unable to see the source of the light.

"Maybe someone should stand watch," Margo suggests.

"No, haven't you ever watched a horror film? Never split up," I respond.

"We're in this together. Whatever it is," Tahlia adds.

We cautiously enter through a narrow passageway, feeling the cool dampness of water dripping from the loose old bricks. A foul-smelling stream of water trickles along the center of the tunnel, forcing us to split into separate sides. It's not ideal, but I can still see Tahlia and Riley, and it's probably better they're the two that parted from us.

Jessa's shrill scream reverberates through the tunnel, confirming our location. In perfect synchronization, we exchange glances, and the five of us dart through the tunnel.

Riley's light speeds ahead of us.

"What the hell have you done?" The piercing sound of Riley's startled howl fills the tunnel.

CHAPTER 39
THE CHOSEN ONE

Jessa emits another bloodcurdling scream, but it's cut short.

Something is very wrong.

My legs struggle to keep up with the others as I rush through the tunnel, causing me to fall behind and lose sight of them.

My friends' collective ear-piercing wails send a jolt of adrenaline through my veins. My new pace becomes frantic, and I lose control of my speed, crashing into Riley's solidly planted body. The impact propels me backward, causing me to land in a shallow puddle of murky water. As I struggle to get back on my feet, I'm accosted with the sight of Jessa's straight, platinum blonde hair cascading down from her limp body on a table.

Blood is weaved through her hair like terribly placed lowlights.

The rise and fall of her chest is barely noticeable. It's enough to confirm she's still alive, but that still doesn't tell us who did this to her.

My foot keeps slipping every time I try to get up.

"It's about time," a familiar voice says.

Through Riley's legs, I manage to steal a quick glance at the person speaking, catching sight of their feet, but nothing more.

"What the hell is going on?" Riley demands. "Sam, what have you done?"

His words send me slipping back into the shallow water. *Sam?*

Callen reaches down, and with a firm grip, he pulls me up.

Sam Hornsby's unmistakable figure now dominates my view as he stands over Jessa, who is tightly restrained on a white table in the center of the tunnel like a scene from a dark and twisted play or musical. It's his stage, and we're his unwilling patrons.

"Jessa!" I scream, the echo of my voice bouncing off the walls of the tunnel.

I lunge forward, but Callen's firm grip keeps me back.

"She can't talk right now. She's taking a little nap," Sam says with a cruel smile plastered across his face.

"Why are you doing this to her?" Tahlia shrieks.

Sam's eyes grow colder with each passing second, drawing out his response, making us wait in torment. "It turns out our little friend here is the reason I spent two months in jail. But you witches already knew that."

He knows. Fear crawls across my skin.

Riley takes a small step forward. "Bro, you don't know what you're talking about."

"This murdering little bitch ruined my life. That's all I need to know." Sam slides a dagger out from under his belt.

Tahlia's breath gets caught in her throat. "Is-is she dead?"

The movement in her chest is slowing, and each breath is taking longer to come.

"Not yet," Sam scoffs, taking the tip of the blade and gently drawing it down Jessa's face.

"What makes you think she had anything to do with it?" I ask.

"Let's just say a little birdie told me." Sam lets out a maniacal laugh.

"But you two have been hanging out," I sputter.

"It's one of those 'keep your friends close, but enemies' closer' kind of things, if you catch my drift."

I grit my teeth, thinking back to that day at school in the hallway. I actually felt bad for him. He fooled me.

"It's called acting," Sam says, as if reading my thoughts.

"OK. I get it. You think Jessa had something to do with Megan's death, but why bring her here? What's with all the dramatics?" Tahlia demands.

"This is all part of a bigger plan. I'm just getting what's owed to me—revenge. It's so nice you all came; makes my job so much easier. You even brought the chosen one."

I gulp, my words getting lost in my throat. With my head down, I slowly step forward.

This time, Riley is the one pulling me back.

"Not her." Sam chuckles.

A mixture of confusion and panic fills the air, leaving us all questioning Sam's words.

Not her.

But I'm the chosen one.

"Her." Sam points forward.

My eyes follow his pointing finger to Tahlia and Margo, who are tightly nestled together. The dim light of the tunnel plays off their nervous faces. Fresh tears stream down Margo's face, her cheeks glistening with sadness, while Tahlia's hunter side seems to be activating as her eyes swirl with red.

Is Margo the chosen one?

"He's talking about me," a soft voice comes from behind the group.

Everyone whips around. My ears buzz with the commotion as my eyes strain to make out the figure approaching us. I rub my eyes, and the world around me gradually comes into sharp focus.

"You!" I shout.

Everyone's faces fall heavy with confusion.

"It's her. It's the girl—Scarlet."

CHAPTER 40
SACRIFICE

The girl with long legs, honey-brown hair, and emerald eyes that showed up on my doorstep is real. Suddenly, I don't feel so crazy. Scarlet isn't a ghost, but a real live person.

Riley becomes tense as she comes to a halt beside him. His fingers form a fist until his knuckles turn white—she's a witch.

"I'm the one he wants," Scarlet responds, fidgeting with the ties of her long, dingy overcoat.

The tunnel fills with a symphony of gasps.

Scarlet takes a step closer to Sam, and Riley's fingers loosen next to his side.

"I'm the one this boy is searching for. The one he's leaving messages for all around town," Scarlet says in her soft voice. "I'm the chosen one."

Relief washes over me like rain.

"We don't even know who you are. How could you be connected to this—to us?" Margo asks, her words coming out shaky.

"Right now, you need to trust me." Scarlet extends both

arms out to her sides, like a mother shielding her children from oncoming traffic.

"Our trust doesn't come easy. You're going to have to tell us who you are and why you're stalking me," I demand.

But Scarlet doesn't turn around. Instead, her eyes remain fiercely pinned on Sam.

Tahlia huffs. "We don't have time for this. We need to help Jessa. Why isn't anybody fucking helping Jessa?"

"That's why I'm here. I'm here to help all of you. You must do as I say." Scarlet turns her head over her shoulder to gaze Tahlia in the eye.

Tahlia retreats as if she's obeying orders.

"Sam." The gangly girl takes another step forward. "You don't have to do this. There is another way. I can help you."

"No, this is the only way." Sam glances over his shoulder, staring into the darkness behind him.

"I can help you," Scarlet pleads, pulling his attention back to us.

"No, they said it has to be this way," Sam responds, bitterness and anger seeping into his words. "They showed me what this bitch did to my friend Megan—to me. I saw everything. I know who you all are—what you are!" he screams, leveraging the dagger above Jessa. "This is the revenge they promised me, if I did what they asked."

"Did what who asked?" I cautiously press him.

"The ones that haunt you. I did what they wanted. You're all here. The chosen one's here. We can begin the sacrifice to the Dark Mother, and I can get justice."

He turns around and gazes into the long tunnel behind

him. "I brought you the witches that framed me for the murder of Megan Calhoun just as you requested," he calls into the depths of the tunnel. "The one who's responsible for her death, I bring her to you as sacrifice."

Sacrifice?

Scarlet takes a long inhale, and on the exhale she speaks fast. "Sam is being used by the rival coven, as you call them. Since they can't exist in this realm anymore, they selected Sam as their martyr, using his body to exert their influence. They've been showing him things and whispering in his ear, guiding him to the final piece of their plan. This girl isn't the sacrifice—it's all of you."

Sam turns back to us, his face filled with rage, replacing the gleaming dagger above Jessa's lifeless body as if waiting for direction.

"Are we just going to let him kill her?" Tahlia shouts, lunging forward.

"If anyone takes another step closer, I'm going to slice her throat open. Now if everyone could take a step back." Sam brings the blade to Jessa's neck.

We collectively take a step back.

Scarlet whips around. "Riley, move," she says, inserting herself into his place. "We must unite."

Scarlet grabs my hand and Tahlia's hand. I reach for Callen's, and Margo links with Tahlia until we're a line of witches ready for battle, except for one problem—we don't have our magic.

Riley discreetly marches behind us and over to the side of the tunnel, closest to Callen, his eyes bouncing between us and Sam, ready to attack his friend if necessary.

I can't imagine what's going through his mind right now. The hunter side must be tearing him apart inside. Save the witches or save his friend, Sam.

"She must die first." Sam nods to Scarlet.

"That's fine," Tahlia sneers, whipping her forward like an evil game of red rover.

I yank her back.

"If he kills me, then you'll have no chance of getting your magic back. That's what they want. I can't explain right now, but I'm the final link to your magic. If I die, your magic dies." Scarlet drops Tahlia's hand and unties her jacket.

A black and purple antique pendant necklace dangles across her chest—the missing necklace.

"So, what? You stole the necklace, but it's not yours," Tahlia responds.

When light hits the object, it scatters and sparkles in all directions, yet it doesn't glow. Tahlia is right; this necklace doesn't belong to Scarlet.

Scarlet reaches up and places her hand over the pendant. "You have the one that belongs to me," she says.

"Is that one mine?" Tahlia's voice cracks.

Scarlet frowns. "I'm not sure."

"How do we know you're telling the truth?" Margo asks.

"You don't," Scarlet says with a sigh. "Now take my hand again," she instructs Tahlia.

"Can you all shut the fuck up? I can't think," Sam shouts.

Out of the corner of my eye, I catch Callen nodding to Riley.

"We need to take Sam out," Callen urges.

"He's under their spell," Scarlet responds. "You want to make this right; we can't harm him. This isn't his fault."

"I'm not under any spell," Sam hisses. "I want revenge for Megan and for what was done to me." Spit flies out of his mouth.

"And you think this will make it right? If you kill that girl, then everyone will know you're a murderer and everyone will be right about you," Scarlet responds.

"Well, I guess it's a good thing you all followed me here, since the whole town knows you're a bunch of witches, or they will in due time." Sam laughs. "I'll tell everyone that I attempted to save Jessa, but you manipulated her by bringing her here under false pretenses, catching her off guard, and using her as a sacrificial offering to amplify your coven's power. The whole witch hysteria thing will work seamlessly with my plan. Your coven used the soon to be mayor's daughter as your first sacrifice—oh, it's just icing on the cake and fuel to the fire. Perfection."

Scarlet takes a deep breath. "Sam, I don't think you thought this through. The ones that are showing you things and talking to you want all of them dead"—she points to us—"but they want me dead too. They don't care about that poor girl on that table. They don't even care what happens to you. You were simply a vessel to drive Izzy, Callen, Margo, Tahlia, and me here. That's it. They're done with you. I'm surprised they haven't figured out a way to kill you yet."

Out of the corner of Scarlet's eye, a glimmer sparkles, and with that, a vibration resonates through my body, accompanied by a gradual spread of warmth and energy that slowly travels up my arm.

"Are you starting to choke? Can't feel your legs? Are your fingers tingling?" Scarlet probes Sam.

The blood leaves Sam's face, turning him ghostly white. "What are you doing to me?" he shouts, pulling at the tie around his neck until it hangs loose.

"It's not me; it's the ones that brought you here. I told you they were done with you."

Scarlet turns to me and winks.

Oh, she's good.

Sam's body gives way, and he drops to the ground, pulling in struggled breaths.

"We need to get Jessa," Tahlia exclaims, rushing over to her friend. She quickly unties the ropes that bind Jessa's wrists and ankles to the table.

Sam continues to struggle on the ground next to them.

Riley rushes over to assist.

"We don't have long. Hurry!" Scarlet shouts.

Riley scoops Jessa's lifeless body up, his grip tight on our unconscious friend. Unable to ignore the sticky residue of dried blood on her forehead, he wipes it away with the sleeves of his black suit, holding all her weight with one arm. *Hunter strength.* Her blonde hair cascades down, swaying with each movement.

"We have a problem," Margo says, her voice full of hesitation. "I don't think we're going anywhere."

As Margo tries to move forward, an invisible barrier pushes against her, violently propelling her backward.

I rush to Margo's side and attempt to walk forward with the same result.

"I knew this was too easy," Scarlet says, her shoulders slumping as she hangs her head.

"Did you do this?" Tahlia's words seethe from her mouth covered in faded red lipstick. She corners Scarlet, pressing her against the damp brick walls of the tunnel. "Was this all part of your plan? You're one of them, aren't you? Admit it!"

Scarlet parts her mouth, but the words release from Riley.

"Izzy, watch out!" Riley's voice echoes through the tunnel, the urgency sending chills down my spine.

In a whirlwind of motion, I pivot and find myself face-to-face with Sam, his hand gripping his dagger. A deranged smile tugs at the corner of his lips.

Panic floods my body, and my heart pounds so loudly I swear it's going to burst through my chest. I desperately scan my surroundings for an escape route, but there isn't one.

"Kill her," a ghostly chorus of blended voices whisper.

Before I can react, the blade enters my chest, sliding deep into my ribs. I collapse into the shallow puddle of murky water below.

CHAPTER 41
TIME TO CONFESS

I'm surrounded by the muffled sounds of a scuffle. The faint thuds and grunts paint a chaotic picture around me, but my senses grow cloudier as the darkness sets in, everything coming in and out of focus. As soon as the shock hits me, my hands fly to my chest, feeling the tightness in my muscles around the blade. I reach for the hilt, curling my fingers around it. Warm, sticky blood clings to my skin.

"Don't move it," Callen cries, dropping next to me.

I feel no pain, just a gentle warmth spreading through my insides.

Callen carefully lifts my body and carries me to drier ground, gently placing me on my back. Visions of the girls pressing Scarlet against the wall flicker in and out as I catch blurred glimpses of Sam being forcefully tied to the table. Amid the chaos, the screams become the only audible presence, until the beating of my heart silences everything around me.

I struggle to keep my eyes open, the heaviness of my eyelids pulling them shut.

"Izzy, do you trust me?" Callen's voice trickles down my ear.

I strain my neck, nodding my head as far as it will go.

The pressure of Callen grabbing the hilt stings my body, but it's only temporary. Callen pauses, and I force my heavy eyelids open, only to see his velvety eyes widen in shock.

It must be bad.

"Where did the blood go?" he questions.

I command my hand to move. It grazes my chest; the stickiness is gone.

"Pull it out," Scarlet shouts.

"Don't listen to her," Tahlia hisses, her voice dripping like venom.

But before anyone can react, a rush of normalcy infiltrates my cells, and I sit upright.

"Izzy, what on earth are you doing? Lie down," Callen orders, trying to ease me back, but I resist.

I grab the dagger and forcefully pull it out.

Everyone shrieks.

The blade comes out strikingly clean, no trace of my blood to be found.

"How is that even possible?" Tahlia asks, her grip on Scarlet loosening.

Scarlet wiggles her way through the girls and rushes to my side. "It worked," she exclaims. "The dress—it worked!"

Confusion washes over me.

"The dress? It's from you?" I question.

Scarlet nods proudly. "I put a protection spell on all three dresses. I had a feeling you wouldn't be able to resist the temptation of wearing such a gorgeous garment. I was aware of the potential dangers that awaited us tonight, and I was determined to keep everyone safe."

"What about me?" Callen asks.

"I've watched you, Callen. You don't need protection." Scarlet smiles. "So, now do you trust me?"

"I think you proved your loyalty to us, but you have a lot of explaining to do," I respond.

Scarlet lets her hand hover inches away from the magical forcefield that's keeping us contained. "It will eventually wear off."

"So, now what?" Margo nods to Sam on the table, who's struggling in his restraints.

"He will be fine for now. We need to keep your friend comfortable." Scarlet's eyes shift to Jessa.

"She needs a doctor," Tahlia insists, taking a seat next to her on the stony ground.

Scarlet shakes her head. "There's nothing we can do being trapped in here. I can feel her life force; she's OK. It's like she's in a deep sleep."

Riley takes off his suit jacket and uses it as a pillow for Jessa's head. Callen takes his jacket off and places it over her midsection to keep her warm.

Margo puts her hands on her hips. "Well, I guess we have some time, and you have some explaining to do. Who the hell are you? It's time to confess."

CHAPTER 42
SCARLET'S CONFESSION

I take a seat on a pile of rocks located on the right side of the tunnel, away from the water. The stones are cold against my bare legs, but thankfully smooth from the many years of water erosion. Callen and Margo join me, with Riley keeping his distance, taking his seat atop a large boulder. Pain rests heavily across his face as he's clearly struggling with his inner hunter demons that are probably telling him to attack every witch in this tunnel right now. I'm proud of him for showing so much control. His training with Bree must be helping.

Sam's screams echo through the tunnel, pulling me away from my thoughts.

"He'll be fine. He won't remember any of this when we're done here—neither of them will." Scarlet's head bounces from Sam to Jessa.

I pull my legs close to my body, tucking my knees under my chin. "OK. So, why are you here?"

Scarlet's gaze shifts downward as she tugs at the sleeve of her overcoat, reminding me of the odd girl who showed up on my doorstep, not the brave girl who just saved us. "This is hard."

"Spit it out already," Tahlia says.

Scarlet lifts her head and meets my gaze.

My body instantly warms from our connection.

"I'm here because of you, Izzy," Scarlet softly mutters.

"Me?" I question.

"I didn't come when Isobel needed me, but I came when you called to me in the attic, Izzy."

"I-I called for you?" I ask.

Scarlet nods, her long hair swaying across her face. "It was after the day in the forest. You were in your attic, and you pleaded for help, so I came. I've been watching you all."

"Creepy," Tahlia utters under her breath, while stroking Jessa's hair.

Margo rubs her bare arms. "I'm so confused. Maybe you should start at the beginning. How do you know Isobel?"

Scarlet takes a deep breath and drops onto a stack of rocks in front of us, near the splashing water. She gently folds her hands in her lap, and with a blank expression, she begins. "My name is Scarlet Bradbury. I was born in 1674. In 1692, I was arrested for suspicion of witchcraft."

Riley lifts his brow and cocks his head. "Wait, you're over three-hundred years old? How is that possible?"

Scarlet whips her head to the right, narrowing her emerald gaze on Riley. "I will get to that if you let me continue." She clears her throat and adjusts her coat, pulling it tighter around her body. "So, back to my story. I was tossed into a dirty, rat-infested jail cell to await my testing and trials as a witch. Not everyone who was arrested was a witch, but there were some in there. Most didn't commit the crimes they were accused of, including me, but one person did belong in that cell—Elizabeth Crowley."

Sam's large lantern, our only source of light, flickers at the mention of Elizabeth's name. Eerie shadows crawl along the tunnel walls. I lean into Callen for comfort. Riley's eyes punish me, so I quickly pull away.

Scarlet doesn't skip a beat. "Your ancestors, Lydia, Dinah, and Isobel were in the same coven as Elizabeth, as you already know. However, what you may not fully understand is that before they were accused, Elizabeth harbored resentment toward Isobel for her superior magic and taking the position as the coven's high priestess. She was bitter because she was the one who assembled and discovered all of their powers. If it wasn't for her, they would have wasted their gifts.

"This resentment drove her to embrace the dark side, as she believed it would grant her greater control through the use of the dark magics. She delved into the forbidden practice of necromancy, attempting to summon the dead. Your ancestors started to keep their distance from her, but this only fueled her growing madness.

"It was because of Elizabeth that Isobel found herself behind bars. Elizabeth is the one who killed William Williams, Isobel's first husband. She compelled him to walk off the roof, and of course, his wife was left to take the blame, chalking it up to witchcraft. That's how things worked back then. But it wasn't long before the townsfolk caught wind of Elizabeth's practices, and she also found herself imprisoned with her coven mates.

"During our time in jail, Elizabeth was testing all the prisoners, searching for her new army of dark warriors.

"Your ancestors were afraid of what Elizabeth was capable of, but they also knew their own strengths. I was one of the witches Elizabeth tested, but I failed her test. I was a witch, but I couldn't be coaxed into the darkness like some of the others. Darkness has a way of calling to the weak and greedy souls.

"So, one day, the guards took Elizabeth away for her testing, forcing her to leave behind her black and purple pendant necklace. Seizing the opportunity, Lydia snatched it, convinced she was safeguarding everyone from Elizabeth's malevolent magic. Lydia had it in her mind that the necklace was Elizabeth's talisman and the key to her connection to the darkness. Turns out she was right. It was the only one at that time too. Lydia wore that necklace every day and passed it down to her family to protect, but the story got lost along the way." She pauses and shifts her focus. "Margo, that's why the necklace's story and Lydia Bishop were a complete mystery to you. The stories were simply lost over time."

Margo's head sinks with sorrow.

Scarlet sucks in a deep breath. "Anyway, that same day, Dinah was nearing death and only had days to live, if that. She was so frail that if they didn't act immediately, they were going to die in that jail cell. They recruited me to be their fourth—they called me their chosen one. You must always have four witches to do your most powerful magic. Remember that."

Callen cuts in. "We never heard that story before—we were told the three of them escaped without a fourth because they were so powerful, they didn't need a fourth witch."

"They were trying to protect me by keeping me out of their stories, so no one would come looking. I was caught in the crossfires of Elizabeth's curses nonetheless. Elizabeth wasn't stupid; she knew they needed a fourth to escape. She knew I was their chosen one.

"It wasn't until later that we realized she had used her dark magic to create more necklaces that resembled the stolen one.

"She passed them on to her hand-selected coven of worshippers with strict guidelines to ensure the continuation of her dark rituals. All the necklaces made it out of the jail with her chosen witches," Scarlet explains.

"I appreciate the history lesson, but I don't think I'm understanding yet," Margo says sheepishly. "How did the rival coven become worshipers of the Dark Mother?"

"You need to understand that some things about the urban legends and the tunnels are true. Since the 1800s, people would come here to sacrifice someone as an offering to the dark mother for her blessing and powers, but when the time came, you had to answer her calling.

"Your teacher, the pretty one, Norah Jamison, was the high priestess of your rival coven—she and the others worshiped the dark magics and idolized the image of Elizabeth Crowley, drawing them to this very tunnel.

"Norah Jamison offered her husband as the coven's first offering to the Dark Mother. Elizabeth promised she could teach the rival coven to bring back people from the dead, but Norah and her coven of misfits failed. Norah's husband was never returned to the land of the living. Even with the blood of her husband on her hands, she still kept her faith in the Dark Mother and did her bidding, proving her worthiness to her.

"Isobel knew something was afoot. A storm was brewing. She had kept an eye on the rival coven for some time. She knew they were Dark Mother worshippers. When Norah Jamison tried to get close to Isobel, Isobel let her in. She was smart and played the game well, making Norah think she had the upper hand.

"Isobel contacted me through a spell, similar to your plea, Izzy. Isobel wanted my help with this coven, to fight Elizabeth's dark magic and end it once and for all, but I didn't come, and a hunter got her in the end."

"My dad," Riley mutters.

Scarlet nods and her face falls long. "I failed Isobel. I never wanted to leave my purgatory. It was boring there, especially after Isobel left in 1941, but it kept me safe for centuries." Tears slowly veil over her eyes.

"So, now with one less bloodline witch in the world, Elizabeth was one step closer to completing her task. This is where your rival coven takes the lead, tracking down the necklaces, all except for Margo's. They were aware she had it because of the window spell. That worked to their advantage," Scarlet says.

"So, where exactly is this Dark Mother now? How does she have so much control if she's dead?" Riley asks, his face softening.

"After sacrificing herself to ensure the hunter's curse took effect, Elizabeth ruled the 'in-between world,' as you call it. I think she sold her soul to the devil himself. How else would she have this kind of power? She keeps witches in this hell of a realm until they convert to the darkness. A witch's soul is not safe here."

"Anna. Isobel." Their names escape my lips.

Scarlet bows her head. "Knowing how stubborn a Beswick can be, I know they won't convert, so they'll never be able to pass on"—her eyes flicker—"unless we destroy what Elizabeth started."

"The necklaces?" Margo's hand instinctively rises to her bare chest.

Scarlet strokes the chain of the one hanging around her pale neck. "Elizabeth's intent was that once all the bloodline witches were united again, she would call upon the necklace holders to finish what she, her curses, and her band of hunters failed to do—destroy all the bloodline witches once and for all.

"When Izzy and her dad came to town and all of you came together, it was clear the time had come. That day in the forest, they thought they had everything lined up. They had all the necklaces and were using Anna's body and a necklace to link your dad to the magical sacrifice. The only person missing was me, the chosen one. They thought I'd come to help you all, but they were wrong. I was a coward.

They also didn't think a group of hunters would attack them, as they were tasked with the same job.

"So, in a Hail Mary attempt to please the Dark Mother, they took away their magic?" Riley leaps off his boulder, but still keeps his distance.

Scarlet shakes her head without glancing at Riley. "I'm sure their failure displeased Elizabeth, so that's why the rival coven is still after you."

I use Callen's knee to leverage myself off my rock. I take one slow step toward Scarlet and pause, letting my eyes blaze fiercely into hers. "Why didn't you just come out and tell me who you were when you showed up on my doorstep?"

"I haven't been around people in some time, and I messed up." Scarlet purses her lips together and breathes in deeply through her nose. "I wanted to show you that I shared your fire, but I hurt you. Then I got scared and I ran."

"Then what about that day when I chased after you?" I question.

"I wasn't ready. After freaking you out, I needed more time to gather my evidence and figure things out. You saw me after I watched Sam leave another pentagram. There was no way you would have believed me. I scared Sam off, but I looked guilty. All I wanted was to keep you all safe. You're my kin. I wish I would have behaved better, but I'm here now, and I'm ready to help."

"You're a little late for that," Tahlia quips, nodding to Jessa.

I flash Tahlia a wide-eyed glare. We can't piss off the one person who knows how to help us.

"How do we reclaim our magic and bring an end to this

once and for all?" I ask.

Scarlet sighs. "We have a very small window of time, so we need to act quickly. On the night of All Hallows Eve, as the full moon casts its radiant light, we shall harness its mystical energy to enhance my power and awaken yours. But in order to ensure the success of our plan, we must gather every single witch the necklace showed its glow to," Scarlet responds.

"Why are they glowing now?" Margo asks. "I had mine nearly my entire life, and not once did I see it glow."

"The intent was for the dark army to be called upon when we united. The glow signifies that it's time for them to take us out. However, they never expected that we would be the ones holding the necklaces when that moment arrived. Each remaining necklace serves as a beacon alerting the dark army to the presence of a witch that they must eliminate. It's like a magical failsafe for the bad guys, but it's going to royally backfire on them." Scarlet smirks. "We're going to destroy the necklaces, which will hopefully destroy the final curses and free the souls of the in-between world."

"There's just one more missing piece we need to find in order to make this work." With a gentle touch, Scarlet releases the latch of the necklace, allowing it to fall into her palm.

"This must belong to you." Scarlet passes it to Tahlia.

The excitement and apprehension dancing in Tahlia's eyes swirls with the essence of her ever-changing hunter blood, making my nerves rattle. This is the moment we've all been waiting for. Is Tahlia one of us or does the hunter side get to claim her?

Margo and Callen hop off their rocks and join me standing next to Scarlet. All of us fixate our eyes on Tahlia.

Tahlia reaches out, letting the pendant slip into her hand. She tightly cups it, bringing it close to her chest. She closes her eyes as if making a wish, then slowly withdraws her hand from the pendant. Disappointment etches itself onto her face, weighing down her features. "It's not glowing. The necklace isn't mine. I'm not a witch."

I struggle to keep the tears at bay, blinking them back before they can escape.

Scarlet scrunches up her nose. "If it's not Tahlia's, then it must be your father's, Izzy."

The tears I'm fighting back spill over like a broken dam.

Tahlia passes the necklace to Margo and pounds on the magical field keeping us prisoner. It propels her backward as she cries out, "I need to get out of here. Now!"

CHAPTER 43
KARMA'S A BITCH

Scarlet presses her palm outward, hovering near the invisible barrier. "The vibrations are loosening. They're declining in power."

"Can't you use your magic to bring it down?" Tahlia asks.

"The power of dark magic surpasses that of light magic as it manipulates and bends the laws of nature. It plays by a different set of rules. Here, their magic is potent, fueled by the remnants of death and darkness that permeate deep within these tunnel walls. But it shouldn't be long now; I can feel their magic crumbling."

"What are we going to do with them? Jessa won't tell anyone what happened," Margo says, her voice full of uncertainty. "But Sam, he's a loose cannon."

"Fuck you," Sam hisses.

"We must strip away any trace of magic or witchcraft from their memories," Scarlet says.

I scrunch up my nose. "Wait, so Jessa won't have any idea any of this happened?"

"She won't have any recollection of what happened since

she stepped foot in your house for the first time. You've hung out as far as she's concerned, but anything revolving around magic will be a blank space in her memories," Scarlet responds.

A sickness crosses Margo's face. "And she won't have to live with the guilt of what she's done? I don't think that's right."

The corners of Scarlet's mouth tug downward. "It's the only way for you all to stay safe. Trust me, if there was another way, I'd tell you."

Tears gather in Margo's eyes as she gazes at the motionless figure on the ground.

I reach out and cup Margo's hand in mine, squeezing it tight.

"It's not fair," Margo says under her breath.

"Riley, I need your help," Scarlet calls out. "Hurry and bring Jessa over here. I don't have a lot of energy left. I need to do both of them at the same time." Scarlet makes her way over to Sam.

"You witches are so fucking stupid. You can't erase my memories. I know what you did, and I'll come for all of you," Sam jeers.

Scarlet turns back to look at us and mouths the words, "He won't remember."

Riley gently places Jessa next to the table. Scarlet takes her position in the middle of them, facing us. She reaches for their hands. Scarlet's left hand holds Jessa's limp hand, while her right hand struggles to keep a hold of Sam's. Scarlet closes her eyes and bows her head.

> *"Bind their memories twist and tight*
> *Until they realize there is new light.*
> *I twist them and turn them until they are just right.*
> *I call the past to weave with the present without a fight."*

With each recitation of her spell, the atmosphere around us comes alive, vibrating with her energy and causing the water particles to dance in the air. A tingling sensation whips through my body, but it doesn't last long.

Scarlet pauses. "Margo, I sense there is something you want to add before I close out the spell."

The two of them exchange a knowing glance, as if Scarlet is reading Margo's thoughts. Margo nods and I free her hand from my grasp. With determination, she positions herself confidently in front of the trio. She leans over Jessa, her eyes wild as she delicately touches her earlobe with her finger, tracing a gentle path down the length of her ear before whispering something.

"What's she doing?" Callen murmurs.

I shrug. "I have no clue."

Margo lingers there for a moment, muttering something into Jessa's ear before pulling back and flashing Scarlet a kinked grin.

Together, they finish the spell, saying in unison, "So shall it be."

Sam's resistance fades away, leaving his body lifeless on the table and Jessa's state unchanged.

Tahlia attempts the barrier again, freely gliding through to the other side. "It's down!" she exclaims.

"Perfect timing," Scarlet says, pleased.

"Boys, would you mind assisting Jessa and Sam to his car? I believe it's parked discreetly in the trees where the road bends. It's best if they wake up there together. I mean, they were each other's dates tonight. We can let them question how they ended up there, but it's better than the actual truth."

"Shouldn't Jessa get to a hospital?" Tahlia interjects.

"She's fine, like I've been saying all along. I can feel her life force. Trust me. I have the gift of healing. I was never worried about your friend."

Scarlet, Margo, Tahlia, and I follow the guys, carrying Jessa and Sam out of the tunnel.

"So, where are you staying?" I ask Scarlet.

"Izzy, you know the answer to that."

"You can't be serious. You're staying in that rundown cottage. Why don't you stay at my house?"

"I think it's best I keep a low profile until this is all over, then we'll talk. Meet me on All Hallows Eve where you lost your magic. I trust you'll keep the necklaces safe and inform your father."

I nod.

"Stay safe, witches," Scarlet says, taking long strides in the opposite direction of the forest.

I lean into Margo, looping my arm through hers. "So, what did you say to Jessa when you whispered in her ear?"

"Oh, I told her how she's going to die."

I pull back, stunned. "You what?"

"Well, I planted an idea in her head. I told her she's going to get hit by a drunk driver. It may be tomorrow, it may be in fifty years, but either way, when she's lying on the cold dark pavement, she'll understand that she deserves the death she got. Regardless of whether it actually happens, the paranoia will prevent her from ever driving drunk again."

"Margo!"

"I couldn't let it go, Izzy. Karma's a bitch. What goes around comes around, even if her memories are erased."

CHAPTER 44
THE MISSING LINK

Once again, I'm a prisoner in my bed, fear pinning me in place. I've had an entire week to tell my dad the truth, but I'm a coward. Everyone's depending on me, and I've been nothing but a disappointment. I only have hours until the full moon rises high in the night sky. Today is the day, and I'm dreading it like nobody's business. I don't know how or where to start.

Ugh! I tug my comforter over my head in dread, but a chorus of laughter crawls through my open bedroom door, drawing me out from my sulky solitude and into the hallway.

The curious mixture of voices propels me down the staircase.

"Oh, good, you're awake," Callen says, crossing the foyer, meeting me on the last step.

Am I dreaming?

My tired eyes flutter rapidly, trying to make sense of the unusual activity in my home.

"What's going on? Who's here with you?"

Callen flashes me one of his signature charming grins.

"Everyone's here to support you, Izzy."

"Everyone?" I question.

He reaches for my arm and interlocks it in his, gently coaxing me off the final step. "We know how hard this has been for you." He pauses. "But Izzy, there's something you need to see."

My knees tremble as Callen glides me across the foyer, through the living room and into the dining room, where nearly everyone I know is sitting around our long table.

They all pause and gaze at me when I enter the room.

My face becomes a canvas, displaying my confusion for all to see. "What's everyone doing here?" I ask, my eyes bouncing from one chair to the next.

Barrett, Bree, Tahlia, and Margo are sitting peacefully around my table, sharing a pot of coffee with my dad.

My dad's hands are busy working on something.

"Dad, what are you doing?" I question.

He briefly meets my gaze, then his eyes fall back to the object in his hand. "Oh, this? The clasp on Margo's necklace broke. I'm fixing it for her," he says proudly.

Callen leans in and whispers, "That's not Margo's necklace."

Every hair on my neck stands erect. I feel like the floor is going to open up and swallow me whole—it's time to tell him everything.

My knees go weak like they might give way, and my heart plummets into the pit of my stomach. *I'm not ready. I need more time.* I can't help but feel this isn't right—something isn't right.

Dad has the pendant safely covered in his hand while he

uses his pliers to glide the *broken* clasp back together. "Ta-da! It's fixed." He presents the necklace in the palm of his hand.

It's not glowing.

The final necklace doesn't belong to my dad.

Relief fills me from my feet to my ears.

My dad gently passes the necklace to Margo, without a flicker of magic to be seen.

"Thank you," Margo replies. A hint of sadness crosses over her eyes. I know exactly what she's thinking; we're out of time.

Dad clears his throat. "I'm happy you all stopped by. It's nice to have visitors, but you haven't said why you're all here."

To see if you're the missing link.

Bree smiles and responds, "It's Tahlia's birthday tomorrow. We've been so busy we didn't have time to plan a big party, so we thought we'd gather all of her friends and take them out for breakfast at The Bistro on 4th.

"I hear they have amazing pancakes." My dad grins at Callen.

Callen chuckles. "They sure do."

"We'd love it if both you and Izzy could join us. Let's say in an hour?" Bree says.

A full smile spreads across my dad's face. "That sounds wonderful, doesn't it, Izzy?"

I'm still in shock, my mind racing with disbelief. What just happened? My dad isn't the one we're looking for, so who is?

"Yes, that sounds great," I respond, avoiding eye contact. Instead, my eyes are fixated on Tahlia, who's restless in her chair.

Tahlia snatches the necklace away from Margo's grasp and flees the room. Callen, Margo, and I chase after her.

In the foyer, she squeezes the necklace and cries uncontrollably. "If this doesn't belong to Steven, then who does it belong to? We can't have brunch. We need to find another witch, or I'll become a full-blown hunter by morning."

Tahlia lets the chain slip through her fingers, the pendant swaying from side to side.

My eyes grow wide. "Tahlia! Look!" A tingling sensation of goosebumps travels up and down my arms.

The pendant gives off a soft and radiant glow that fills the room.

"It's you. It's always been you," Margo cheers.

Joyful tears streak down Tahlia's face. "But how?"

"I bet your hunter side was overpowering your witchy side. Each time you touched the necklace, you were enraged. First by me kissing Callen, then when we were stuck in the tunnel. Right now, you were just sad and vulnerable. That's the only thing that makes sense," I respond.

Tahlia's beautiful mossy green eyes light up like a Christmas tree. "This is wonderful news. I still have a chance." She crosses her hands and presses the pendant into her chest. "I still have a chance," she repeats, letting out a deep sigh of relief.

"Happy Halloween, witches," Margo says, a smile lighting up her face as she pulls all of us together in a tight embrace. With our heads pressed closely together, she whispers, "So, are you still planning on telling your dad?"

I shake my head from side to side. "I don't think so. In

my heart, I believe it will only hurt him. There's too much to explain. If he's not a part of this, I don't see the point."

"It's his birthright," Tahlia says softly.

A tear glides down my cheek. "I know, but he's not like us, or there would be another necklace. Even Isobel said he couldn't be called. I think he has an ounce of magic in his blood, but not enough to find joy or comfort in his gift. The rival coven was wrong about him. They didn't need him, and neither do we."

Callen, Tahlia, and Margo pull me even tighter, embracing me until it almost hurts.

"We support you," Margo says.

We slowly release our loving embrace and find ourselves standing side by side in front of the antique Victorian hall tree mirror. Nothing unusual happens—no magic, no messages from the other realm—just four friends who are there for each other, no matter what.

As we stand side by side, Callen instinctively reaches for Margo's hand, who then reaches for mine, and I take hold of Tahlia's hand.

We gaze at our reflections in the mirror, and as we do, we say in unison, "Earth, air, fire, water."

With each element named, we know we're bound together, stronger than ever, and ready to face anything that comes our way.

"The witches of East Gate are back," I add. "Now, let's go break some curses, like the badass witches we are."

"Hell yes!" Tahlia responds.

"But can we get some pancakes first?" Callen smirks.

CHAPTER 45
FRIENDS

Outside The Bistro on 4th, Tim and Riley round the corner, nearly bumping into my dad and me.

"Tim. Riley. I didn't know you were coming," I say.

"Yeah, last-minute invite." Riley rubs the back of his neck. His eyes showcase their baby blue today, giving me a slight sense of ease.

"I think everyone was a last-minute invite." My dad chuckles, extending his hand to Tim. "It's been a while. It's good to see you."

As their hands meet in a handshake, I want to shout and scream, *he killed your family*, but that's a secret I have to bury down deep. I made my decision, and I have to stick to it— to protect him from this beautifully twisted and sometimes dark world.

"Sorry, man. The station has me so busy with everything that's been going on around town," Tim responds.

I glare, giving my gaze of caution to Tim. *I'll kill you if you hurt my dad.*

Tim respectively nods as if hearing my threat.

"I must be living under a rock because I have no idea what you're talking about." Dad chuckles while holding the door of the restaurant open for everyone to enter. "We have a lot of catching up to do," he tells Tim as he passes through the door.

Riley pauses. "I need to talk to Izzy. We'll be behind you," he says to our dads.

My heart doesn't immediately leap for joy; instead, fear and apprehension wrap tightly around my heart, squeezing until near suffocation.

"Is it safe for us to be alone together?" I ask as he guides me around the building to a tiny white bench.

He gestures for me to take a seat. "I think so. I'm having a good day today. My training is going well. Bree's been very helpful, but all that might not matter after tonight."

"Speaking of tonight, I can't believe Bree and Tim are on board with this plan," I say.

"They're not."

"What do you mean? Bree was at my house this morning testing my dad with the rest of them. You're telling me she has no idea we're about to break the curses?"

"That's right. They have no idea about the plan, and it's going to stay that way. They think you're only trying to get your powers back. If they knew, do you really think they'd let this happen? They like being hunters. But this is for their own good. I don't want this. I don't think my mother wanted this either. I think that's why she left—she couldn't bear knowing what I'd turn into—my father. I'm going along with this for the good of those who never got a choice."

"Wow, I had no idea. I feel so out of the loop."

"You've had a lot to deal with this week. Everyone thought it was best to let you be."

I grin. "So, you might be back to your old self again by tomorrow morning?"

"Here's hoping everything works as planned. I wish I could be there tonight, but I know it's best if I'm not." Riley's head drops, and his sandy brown hair swoops over his left eye. He pulls in a deep breath and sighs. "Izzy, I'm not going to fight for you anymore."

I open my mouth, but he puts his finger up.

"Let me finish."

My lips fall shut, obeying his request, while my nerves tingle with anticipation. *Where is this going?*

He twists on the bench until our knees touch. "I've had a crush on you since we were little. I loved being at your Gran-gran's house and causing trouble all over town with you. I looked forward to seeing you every summer. When I found out you were back in town for good, I couldn't wait to see you. I was nervous that things would be different, and they were. I turned out to be a hunter"—he shifts his gaze to his fidgeting hands—"and you're a witch." He sighs again; this time it's longer and more drawn out. "We were never meant to be."

"But Bree and Barret?"

"Izzy, we're not like them. As much as I want that to be us, especially with things changing tomorrow, that's not our future. And you're not available."

"What do you mean?"

"It's never been me, Izzy. You and I were a dream we both created to escape the world we lived in. Now that I'm able to think a little clearer, I know it's Callen. I see how the two of you are together. He's your soulmate—I'm your past—the two of you belong together. It would be selfish of me not to recognize that."

He gently kisses my forehead. "I'm letting you go, Izzy."

"Riley," I stammer.

"It's OK. I don't want you to hang onto this guilt. I want you to be happy."

"I want you to be happy too."

He stands up, turns back to me, and smiles. "I know you do." He pivots to walk away.

"Wait," I call out. "Can we still be friends?"

"I'd like that very much. See you inside, friend."

CHAPTER 46
AS ABOVE SO BELOW

The sky cracks with lightning, filling the air with a sudden burst of brightness and revealing the full moon peeking through the breaks in the dark clouds.

"Here goes everything," Callen says, leading me into the forest.

Barrett, Tahlia, and Margo are trailing behind.

The wind moans mournfully through the bare branches of the trees, making them sway and shudder. The gusts bring more leaves down to the ground, adding to the thick layer that already covers the damp earth.

As Callen and I trudge through the leaves, I'm reminded that the coldest and darkest days are yet to come. But despite the looming threat of death and decay, somehow, things always move forward, and greener times are around the corner. I can be just as resilient as the earth's cycles and take comfort knowing that spring will come again and so will our happiness, no matter what happens here tonight.

As if summoned by the moon itself, Scarlet emerges from behind a towering oak tree. We continue our journey in complete silence until we finally reach the spot where the rival coven cursed us.

"I never thought I'd find myself in this place again," I whisper to Callen, feeling the warmth of his hand intertwined with mine.

"Me neither." He squeezes tight.

The haunting scent of death remains imprinted in my mind, evoking a visceral reaction as I walk through our former war zone.

Margo carefully places a bundle of vibrant sunflowers she carried in with her on the spot where her mother tragically lost her life. "They were her favorite flower." She smiles, dropping to her knees.

Callen, Scarlet, Barrett, and I give Margo her space and begin setting up by carefully drawing a salt circle, purifying the area with white sage, and arranging our offerings. One offering is soil taken from the unmarked graves of the persecuted witches in Salem that Scarlet retrieved earlier this week. She said it would amplify her magic.

Once Margo rejoins us, we distribute the necklaces, each pendant basking in a unique glow as we secure them around our necks.

Scarlet brings the blade of our dagger to her hand and makes an incision, letting her blood flow into our bowl. We take turns until the offering is complete. She nods her head and extends her hands for us to grab, signaling that it's time.

As we converge into a unified coven, the sky reverberates with a mighty roar, and the billowing clouds disperse, unveiling a radiant full moon that casts a celestial glow over our sacred gathering.

In our circle, our bond is unbreakable. An immense strength courses through me, like a tidal wave crashing against the shore. The necklaces around our necks emit a more intense mesmerizing glow and we begin.

"Earth, air, fire, water," we chant in rounds as the air circulates around us and grows lighter by the second.

The desire to experience the comforting touch of my fire intensifies. So far, I only feel the pulsating vibrations of Scarlet's magic infiltrating my cells and extending into Callen, connecting us all in a continuous loop. I hold no power of my own.

Scarlet takes a deep breath and recites her spell from memory.

"Hail to the guardians of mother earth, air, fire, and water."
We come to you with a tide of offerings
In hopes of ending our sufferings.
Guide their magic back to where it belongs.
Take the curses and right the wrongs.
Restore the lightness where there is dark.
They shall leave no mark.
Pull the blood that taints the hunters
And fix this magical blunder.
We ask for light to guide our souls
And close all the empty holes.
As above, so below."

I raise my eyes to the sky. I'm captivated by the stark contrast between the darkening right side and the left side, aglow with a soft, golden radiance. A turbulent blend of sickness and fire courses through my body. The contrasting forces of darkness and light engage in a war, asserting their dominance over me—over us—and over nature itself.

A menacing energy presses against our protective barrier. The sinister voices of the rival coven lash through the air, attempting to provoke us, but we remain steadfast. Within our sacred space, they have no power over us.

Scarlet repeats her spell, and my magic hums in my bones, waiting to be released. Hopeful smiles spread across our faces, and I know my coven mates are experiencing the same sensation.

There's hope.

We join Scarlet with the final recitation of her spell. Electricity flows rapidly through my body, nearly knocking me to the ground, but I squeeze Callen's hand to keep myself firmly planted in place.

My magic pulsates within me, eager to be unleashed, desperate to find its place within my body and soul. In unison, we close out our spell, our final plea to the universe— to mother earth, air, fire and water. "So shall it be."

The brilliant glow of our necklaces radiates a path of light that grows, extending and reaching until it blends into a single luminous trail. Then it stretches and merges into a dazzling beam before exploding into the sky, causing the pendants around our necks to shatter.

The cells inside my body tingle as if they're multiplying. Heat surges through my fingertips, traveling swiftly up my arm and settling in a fiery warmth across my chest. The darkness in the sky above dissipates, making way for the serene expanse of the calmness that settles over us. The devilish voices are gone.

I glance to Callen, Tahlia, Margo, and Barrett, their faces aglow with satisfaction.

Our hands remain intertwined as a circle. Each of us gaze into each other's eyes, appreciative for what we accomplished.

Gratitude fills me up. "We did it!" I exclaim, my voice choked with tears. "We're finally free from the grip of the rival coven's curse. I feel my fire. Our magic's back."

Tahlia's the first to break our circle, her hands releasing from her dad and Margo's hold. She desperately removes her coat and sweater. Standing in the cold, with only a tank top on, we watch as her delicate hunter tattoo slowly fades away on her arm.

Tears flush from Tahlia's eyes. "We did it. I'm free. We broke the hunter's curse." She falls to her knees and presses her palms into the ground. "Thank you." She rises and places her hands on her temples as she gazes at the full moon.

Everyone surrounds Tahlia, following her lead as we join her in gazing at the moon and giving thanks to the elements for what we received.

Barrett pulls Tahlia into a tight hug, holding her in his arms. He gives Callen a pat on the shoulder before turning his attention to Scarlet. "We couldn't have done this without you. Thank you for coming." He pivots. "Sorry to get my magic back and run, but my wife is going to freak. I need to get home and explain, but I know this is for her own good. She will eventually understand—I hope."

"We got this, Dad. Go home to Mom. We'll be home shortly," Callen says.

Barret disappears into the deep forest.

"So, Scarlet, what's your plan now that you're a free woman in the twenty-first century?" Margo asks.

"I think I'd like to stick around East Gate for a while," Scarlet responds, bending down to gather our supplies.

Margo skips through the center of our circle. Stopping in front of me, she mouths, "She's cute, right?"

I giggle and nod my head.

Callen clears his throat, drawing my attention to him. "You." He points at me.

"Me?" I playfully respond.

He gives me a smirk, and I hear the words in his head. "It's you and me, Beswick. Kindred spirits, always and forever."

My lips curve into a smile so quickly that my mind can barely keep up with my emotions. The rapid thumping of my heart reverberates through my chest, and my stomach fills with a flurry of happiness.

I run toward him, throwing myself into his arms. I gaze into his velvety eyes. "Oh, Callen, it's you. It's always been you."

"You're my end game, Izzy Beswick."

EPILOGUE
SIX MONTHS LATER

"Are you going to open it?" Margo waves a white envelope addressed to me in the air.

Callen places his hand on my shoulder. "Are you just going to stand here and leave us in suspense? Take the letter." He nudges me forward, but I don't move.

Tahlia leaps up from the couch, crosses the room, snatches the letter from Margo's hands, and places it next to me. "Just open the dang thing."

It turns out all her angst wasn't just the hunter blood; it's who Tahlia is. But I kind of like that about her now. Her mossy green eyes stare me down, waiting for me to react.

The anticipation is too overwhelming. I can't bring myself to open the envelope—what if I don't get in? I know my friends are just as nervous as me to find out whether I'll be joining them at the same school. It would royally suck if I'm the only one who didn't get in. Would Callen, Margo, and Tahlia all leave me behind? After we restored our magic, we devised a plan, and if I don't get in, it will ruin everything.

"I'm too nervous. I can't do it. What if I don't get in?" I

sputter.

"Sweetie, I'm sure it's an acceptance letter," Dad reassures me.

That's what he's supposed to say.

"You do it," I forcefully push the letter back into Margo's hands.

With zero hesitation, Margo eagerly tears into the envelope. Her eyes narrow as she scans the page, her unreadable expression causing my stomach to knot with anxiety. Too much of our future is riding on this letter. I don't want to disappoint my friends and boyfriend.

The corners of her mouth slowly tug upward. "You got in!" Margo exclaims, passing me the letter.

I have to blink a few times to convince myself that I'm not imagining it, but the words on the page are crystal clear for everyone in the room to see.

Dear Isobel Beswick,

We are pleased to inform you of your acceptance to Salem State University.

Everything else on the page is a blur, but I did it. I got into college. Waves of relief course through my veins, invigorating me with calmness. I know it's not a college for witches because that would be crazy if those existed, but it's the next best option for us. I can't wait to be closer to where the magic started and dive deeper into our heritage, returning to the place that birthed our ancestor's powers.

I also got accepted to The University of Connecticut, but that never felt like the right place for me. I knew there was something better for me, and there is—SSU.

"It's official!" Callen gleams. "We're all going to college together!" He does a silly happy dance in front of me, and I can't help but blush.

"I still wish you had chosen to stay in state, but I'm happy for all of you. However, I'm going to miss you terribly. I hope you'll come back and visit your old dad from time to time. Don't forget about me."

"Um, hello! I could never forget about you, Dad."

A soft but delighted smile falls across my dad's face.

An eruption of cheer and chatter fills the room.

"What's the commotion?" Scarlet asks, rounding the corner in her new red robe, clutching a steaming cup of coffee in her favorite yellow mug.

"Izzy got into Salem State University," my dad responds, his eyes overflowing with pride.

"Izzy, that's so wonderful." Scarlet sips her steaming beverage, taking a seat next to Margo.

"Scarlet, I think you have an addiction to the brown stuff," Margo jokes.

It's true. That girl's addicted to coffee. It's hard to believe she never had it until Callen got her a job at The Perk. Now it's all she drinks.

Scarlet laughs. "It's only my third cup of the day."

"Did I hear Izzy got her acceptance letter?" Jonathan asks, entering the room with a large red toolbox in tow.

"You heard right," Dad responds, standing up. "I'm

proud of you, kiddo." He kisses the top of my head. "I hate to leave this happy little celebration, but Jonathan and I have to work on the west wing bedrooms today if we're going to officially open the B and B in three months."

"It's so cool you're opening Beswick Manor up as a bed-and-breakfast," Callen says. "I can't believe how much things have changed around here in six months. This place looks amazing."

"I couldn't have done it without my right-hand man." Dad nods to Jonathan. "I'm so grateful he's in our lives."

And I'm grateful that Jessa's dad lost the election to a write-in candidate—Barret Hart—putting an end to the unnecessary witch hunt, so I could get on board with my dad and Jonathan's crazy and out of nowhere idea.

Tahlia twirls the wild loose curl that always manages to slip out of her messy ponytail. "Mr. Beswick—"

"Tahlia, it's Steven, remember?" my dad cuts her off.

She laughs. "Right, *Steven*," she enunciates his name. "Are you planning on working and running the B and B? That's a lot to take on."

My dad breaks into a sly grin. "I think it's high time I break the exciting news that besides already being an ideal investor and partner, Jonathan will be moving in as the full-time innkeeper and handyman. This way, I can continue to work and bring in a steady income until things take off. It will be nice to have the extra income from the B and B to help pay for Izzy's schooling."

"I'm almost retired, anyway. I have nothing in West Gate keeping me there, so I may as well help out my son and keep an eye on my investment." Jonathan winks at us.

Everyone congratulates them on their news, and I nod in approval of their plan. I love that my dad and Jonathan have grown close. I can't help but think Anna's happy wherever she may be. Her son found his father, and it's like they've been in each other's lives forever.

"It's nice to have a house guest to practice on," Dad says, pulling my attention back to the room.

I can't help but smile at how easily everything came together after Halloween. The moment they laid their plan on me, I suggested my new friend Scarlet, *who just moved to town*, was in need of a place to stay. I convinced them she'd make the perfect first guest to help them work out the kinks in their plan. Scarlet's been living with us as a long-term guest in the east wing since that day. She's even helped me clean up the attic and find better hiding places for our magical supplies. I couldn't keep that room hidden from my dad forever.

"I'm eternally grateful for your kindness," Scarlet says, cozily cupping her coffee in her hand.

Sitting here in my living room, I can't help but smile as I gaze at the family I've built. Family isn't defined by bloodline; it's about the individuals you've carefully chosen as your loved ones. I even consider some ex-hunters part of my family, like Bree and Riley—never Tim, though. It's hard to hate a man who had no control over his actions. It wasn't Tim who killed my family; it was the hunter's curse. I realize that now, but it's still a hard one to get over.

It was surprising to discover that the hunters, once freed

from their curse, showed no interest in retaliation. Instead, they felt free and happy without the burden of their hate-fueled desire to hunt in their hearts.

As for Jessa, she still comes around, but things aren't the same. She and I never truly bonded because we didn't have the same shared experiences anymore. And even though she doesn't remember what happened that night in August in her white Jeep on the dark highway road, we know the truth, and Margo can never forgive her for that.

Things have even worked out for Sam Hornsby. He's been exonerated in the court of public opinion, due to the discovery of a letter in Mrs. Jamison's house confessing to Megan's death and implicating Robin as well, stating their plans to flee town. We might have had something to do with that.

People have turned Dale and Darla and their store, Invoke Awakenings, into something of a new urban legend. I mean, it's hard not to when two creepy siblings up and vanish, leaving their store behind. That's how urban legends and stories start, right?

Don't mess with the Witches of East Gate.

Jonathan clears his throat, drawing my attention back to the room. "Izzy, during the process of dismantling your bedroom wardrobe to make way for your new closet, I came across a letter taped to the inside, addressed to you." He hands me a small red envelope before heading out of the room with my dad and his toolbox in hand.

I take a deep breath and unfold the note, keeping it for my eyes only.

Our dearest Izzy,

We're proud of you.

My heart and tingling fiery feeling assure me that the note, despite lacking a signature, is from Anna and Isobel, giving me a sense of peace and closure.

I'm a Beswick and proud of it.

A firm knock flows into the living room. "That's Riley," Tahlia says, a grin plastering her face as she leaps to her feet. "I hope you don't mind that I invited him over."

"Of course not," I respond.

Callen comes up from behind me and whispers in my ear. "I still can't believe the two of them ended up together."

I smile. "I can."

Everyone has a soulmate, and Tahlia is Riley's. She's been protecting him since the day I met her. It's funny how two hearts can be so intricately intertwined that they find each other, no matter what obstacles are thrown in their way.

I giggle at the thought and stare at *my* soulmate. His velvety gaze still has a mesmerizing effect on me, melting my heart each time our eyes meet.

"What, Beswick? You've got a funny grin on your face."

I bite my bottom lip. I know my cheeks are blushing. "Nothing. I'm just really happy."

"Me too, Beswick." He leans in and gives me a sweet kiss on my reddening cheeks.

"I'm getting bored. Let's do something," Margo says,

leaping to her feet, tugging on Scarlet's arm to join her.

"All right. What should we do?" Callen asks.

A mischievous smirk spreads across Margo's face. "Is anyone up for a game of light as a feather?"

I laugh. "I thought you would never ask."

The End.

ACKNOWLEDGMENTS

First, I want to express my deepest gratitude to all my readers who have supported me throughout the journey of writing this series. Your words of encouragement and enthusiasm have inspired me greatly, and I couldn't have done it without you. So, from the bottom of my heart, thank you. You are the reason I get to keep writing stories.

I also want to thank my husband, Jeremy, for his unwavering support of my author career. I'm fortunate to have such a supportive partner in my life. Without you, none of this would be possible. Thank you for keeping me level-headed and reminding me that it's okay to take breaks. You know what I need before I do sometimes.

A big thank you also goes out to my amazing editor, Nichole Heydenburg, at Poisoned Ink Press. Your feedback and advice have been invaluable to me, and I appreciate all the hard work you put into making me a better writer.

I am also grateful to my talented cover designer, Natasha MacKenzie. Every cover you've designed for this series is outstanding, and I couldn't be happier with how they turned out. You are genuinely brilliant.

To my sisters, Sarah and Rachel, thank you for being the incredible people you are. You are my forever coven, and I am so grateful to have you in my life.

I want to extend my gratitude to my mom and Don, Dad and Emily, and Pam and Bryan. Your support means the world to me! A special thanks to Pam and Emily for being the last set of eyes on this book before publication.

To my critique partner and accountability buddy, Stacey Spangler, thank you for keeping me on track with our weekly chats and daily check-ins.

To my other writer friends, including the Thriller Babes, thank you for your support, encouragement, and knowledge.

Finally, I thank my street team, betas, and ARC readers for your support. I'm so lucky to have you all on my team. I've met so many wonderful people while working on this series.

I hope you all enjoyed the Dark Magic Series, and once again, thank you to everyone who believed in me and my dreams. I couldn't have done it without you!

ABOUT THE AUTHOR

Jamie Lee Fry is an Oregon-based author with Iowa roots who enjoys creating dark, captivating, and fast-paced stories. When Jamie's not hunched over her desk plotting her next thrilling novel, she's hiking in the mountains with her husband Jeremy and their two dogs. Jamie never says no to a good adventure as long as mountains and waterfalls are involved. Jamie loves documenting life with her camera. She also enjoys stand-up paddleboarding, kayaking, cross-country skiing, baking, and consuming copious amounts of coffee.

CONNECT WITH JAMIE

Scan the QR code above, or visit:

@Author_JamieLeeFry
www.authorjamieleefry.com